"I'll just wipe his paws with a damp cloth so he doesn't track up the floor. He and his mama can do the rest."

Moving slowly and murmuring endearments to the frightened kitty, Belinda made her way to the sink. Cradling the kitten against her with one hand, she turned her attention back to Paul and began to dab at the faint, tiny paw prints on his T-shirt with a damp towel.

"Leave it alone. It's okay," he said.

"It'll just take a second...." she protested.

Paul's hand closed around hers, stilling her efforts.

Confused, Belinda raised her eyes to meet his. He didn't speak. He didn't have to. The look in his eyes was enough.

Books by Valerie Hansen

Love Inspired

The Wedding Arbor #84
The Troublesome Angel #103
The Perfect Couple #119
Second Chances #139

VALERIE HANSEN

was thirty when she awoke to the presence of the Lord in her life and turned to Jesus. In the years that followed she worked with young children, both in church and secular environments. She also raised a family of her own and played foster mother to a wide assortment of furred and feathered critters.

Married to her high school sweetheart since age seventeen, she now lives in an old farmhouse she and her husband renovated with their own hands. She loves to hike the wooded hills behind the house and reflect on the marvelous turn her life has taken. Not only is she privileged to reside among the loving, accepting folks in the breathtakingly beautiful Ozark mountains of Arkansas, she also gets to share her personal faith by telling the stories of her heart for Steeple Hill's Love Inspired line.

Life doesn't get much better than that!

Second Chances
Valerie Hansen

Published by Steeple Hill Books™

STEEPLE HILL BOOKS

Steeple
Hill™

ISBN 0-373-87146-5

SECOND CHANCES

Printed in U.S.A.

Blessed are the peacemakers;
for they shall be called the children of God.
—*Matthew 5:9*

This book is dedicated to all the special people
whose calming influence and wise counsel
brings daily peace to all our lives.

Prologue

An orange glow danced across the night sky. Flames curled around the three-storey frame structure, licking the thick layers of old paint and bubbling them to ashes, then consuming the dry wood beneath. Firelight radiating through the window of eighteen-year-old Belinda Carnes's bedroom turned the pale pink interior walls a sickly yellow.

Shocked awake, she bolted out of bed, ran to the window and stared at the fire next door. In the street below, her father was shouting, pleading, "Somebody do something. Dear God, do something!" The sound of his anguish tore at her heart, making her temporarily forget the terrible quarrel they'd had only hours before.

"Daddy!" Grabbing her robe, Belinda made a dash for the stairs. Their house was full of smoke, making it difficult to see or breathe. Maybe it was on fire, too!

She rocketed into the street, auburn hair flying, her robe clutched around her slim body, her feet bare. "Daddy! Where are you?"

The first fire truck was already shooting water on the flames as others arrived. "Get back!" someone shouted. Belinda ignored the order. She had to find her father. He was all she had left.

A team of volunteer firefighters ran by, dragging a bulging hose. Several of the men were part of her father's congregation. Gasping to catch her breath, Belinda looked at the church that had been her second home since before her mother had died. She didn't have to know much about firefighting to know the historic building, her father's pride and joy, was beyond saving.

Blossoming spray from the hoses drifted over the appalled onlookers like icy mist over a river. Wending her way through the crowd, Belinda overheard more than one angry person place the blame for the terrible inferno on Paul Randall, the misfit teenage son of a convicted arsonist.

They were wrong. They had to be. She was sure Paul had left town right after her father had ordered him out of their house and out of her life for good. The bitterness of that altercation echoed in her throbbing head.

"Leave my daughter alone," her father had shouted just hours ago.

Paul had stood his ground, feet planted firmly apart on the front walkway, fists clenched in defiance. "We're in love. We're going to get married, with or without your blessing. There's nothing you can do about it."

"We'll see about that."

"I'm leaving town tonight and Belinda's coming with me," Paul had said flatly.

"No, she isn't." Her father had held out his hand to her, his commanding voice as forceful as if he were warning his congregation about the wages of sin. "Belinda is going to go away to college in the fall, just like she promised her mother. By the time she gets her degree she'll be wise enough to make the kind of choices that will affect her whole life. Right now, she's far too young."

Caught between her vow to her late mother and the angry young man who insisted they marry immediately and run away together no matter what the consequences, Belinda had felt trapped. Weeping, she'd stepped to her father's side. No words were necessary. Her actions had spoken for her.

"Fine. I'll go," Paul had yelled, cursing to accentuate his mood. "But I'll show you. You'll be sorry. You'll *both* be sorry. You just watch."

Even now, Belinda imagined she could still hear the echo of Paul's vehement threats. When he'd lost his temper and threatened her father she'd glimpsed a side of him she'd never seen before. A part of his character that had truly frightened her. And now the church was on fire. Thank goodness Paul was long gone! If he were still in town, he'd be the first one *she* suspected, too.

Belinda was so distraught she could hardly breathe, hardly think. Blinking back tears, she worked her way through the twisted maze of hoses lying in the street. Behind her, the upper windows of the old church began to shatter from the intense heat and the pressure of the water being hurled against them.

As she drew closer to her father she saw two men restraining him to keep him from trying to enter the burning building. "Thank you, God. He's safe," she whispered, grateful beyond belief.

All she could think about was getting to her father so she could tell him how sorry she was about the church and how much she loved him, in spite of their recent argument.

Suddenly, strong, masculine hands grasped her from behind. Held her fast. Told her, "It's not safe to be out here barefoot."

Panicking, Belinda twisted to stare at him. Her eyes widened. It *couldn't* be Paul...but it was. She immediately tried to jerk free. "Let go of me!"

Scowling, Paul released her, held his hands in the air and took a step back. When he said, "Sorry," it sounded a lot more like sarcasm than penitence.

"What are *you* doing here?"

"I heard the sirens so I came by to make sure you were all right."

Fire reflected in the depths of his almost-black eyes, making him appear sinister, dangerous. Belinda's already broken heart hardened at the sight of him, at the realization that all her wonderful excuses for his innocence were useless now that she knew he was still hanging around the area. "Stop lying, Paul," she countered. "You came here to gloat and you know it."

He combed his fingers through his long, thick, dark hair, pushing it back as he shook his head. "You have a really low opinion of me, don't you?"

"I only know what I see. You said you were leaving town hours ago. Why didn't you *go?*"

Paul's jaw clenched, but he kept his outward cool. "I was packing. I knew your father banished me from this town but I didn't know he was timing me or I'd have hurried."

"Leave my daddy out of this. Haven't you done enough to hurt him already?"

"Me? Hurt *him?* All I did was fall in love with his daughter!"

Paul saw Belinda's tear-filled glance dart briefly in the direction of the burning church before returning to him. Suddenly understanding, he nodded. "I should have known. I thought you were different but you're just like the rest of them, aren't you?" His arm swept in an arc that took in the whole chaotic scene. "You blame me for this. All of you do." He shoved his hands into the pockets of his worn leather jacket. "It figures. My father made a mistake and went to prison for arson, so I'm guilty by association. Right?''

The unfair accusation stung, made her even more defensive. ''You said it. I didn't.'' Standing firm, she refused to let him off the hook. ''You were supposed to be long gone by now. Admit it. You only hung around so you could watch my father suffer.'' Pent-up emotion made her tremble. ''Get away from me! I never want to see you again. Ever.''

''Fine with me. I'm glad your old man decided that I'm not good enough for you. He did us *both* a favor. Goodbye, Belinda. Have a nice life.''

With tears running down her cheeks, Belinda pressed her fingertips to her lips to stifle her sobs as she watched Paul elbow his way through the throng of hostile onlookers, mount his motorcycle and roar away. She realized she was saying goodbye to more than Paul Randall. She was also giving up the naive belief that her love was enough to change him, to save him from the negative effects of his dysfunctional upbringing.

Admitting she'd been wrong about him was breaking her heart.

Chapter One

Belinda Carnes was busy sorting local business files in the tall cabinet at the rear of her office when she heard the familiar ding of the electric eye that monitored the front door. She smoothed her skirt and breezed around the corner into the reception area with an expectant smile, recognizing her visitor immediately. "Sheila! Hi."

"Aren't you going to say, 'Welcome to Serenity. How can the Chamber of Commerce help you'?"

"Nope. I save that speech for the tourists." Belinda's smile widened. "And I leave out the part about the ticks and chiggers eating us alive all summer. What's up?"

"You mean you haven't heard?"

"Heard what? What are you talking about?"

"He's back."

"Who's back?" The fine, auburn hair at the nape of Belinda's neck began to prickle.

"Don't play dumb with me," Sheila said. "You know very well who I mean. Verleen saw that lawyer, Paul Randall, coming out of the market downtown. He'd been buying groceries. Bags of them. I'd say that means he plans to stay with those ancient aunts of his for quite a while."

Belinda blinked rapidly and paused to digest her friend's comments. The whole idea of Paul being anywhere nearby tied her stomach in knots, made her pulse speed. "I'd heard he was going to help the Whitaker sisters with the legalities of their real estate deal but I didn't think he'd actually come here to do it. What gall."

"What do you mean?"

"It's a long, complicated story." She sighed. "Let's just say Paul didn't turn out to be the wonderful guy I thought he was."

"Oh? What makes you say that?"

"You mean you haven't heard the gossip yet? Amazing. The way rumors fly in this town, I'd have thought you'd already know the whole story."

"I'd rather hear it straight from you," Sheila said with undisguised interest.

Belinda filled her in concisely, trying to leave out any supposition. She concluded with, "No one has ever proved who was—or wasn't—responsible for setting fire to the church...but nobody had any real motive except Paul."

"Wow. No wonder you don't want to come face-to-face with him."

"I'm glad you understand."

"Yeah, well…" A sly smile lifted Sheila's lips. "That's really too bad. I hear Randall is the best-looking guy around. And rich. I was kind of hoping you might want to introduce me to him. There aren't that many eligible men in this area, you know."

Belinda was flabbergasted. "You'd be interested in him, even after what I just told you?"

"Why not? Lots of us do crazy things when we're teenagers. It looks to me like he's reformed."

Shaking her head, Belinda made a face at her friend. "Not reformed. Just turned his talents to getting back at Serenity by legal means. Don't forget the lawsuit against the town fathers a few years back. When he proved land-use discrimination and the councilmen had to back down, they all lost face. Half of them weren't reelected."

"So? That's just business."

"Not in a close-knit town like this one. Around here, it's considered a vendetta. That's another reason I don't want anything to do with him."

"Guilt by association, you mean? I'm surprised you don't already have a problem with that. I hear that you used to tell everybody you were going to marry Paul."

Belinda blushed. "I was just a high school kid with a stupid crush on the only boy in town my father refused to let me date. In other words, a typical teenager. Besides, that was ten years ago. Believe me, I'm cured and everybody knows it...especially me."

"Being young doesn't mean you can't fall in love for keeps," Sheila countered. "My mom got married when she was seventeen. She and Dad are still doing okay."

"My parents had a wonderful relationship, too. Everything changed when my mother died, though. The only thing that saved Daddy's sanity was focusing all his energy on his church."

"The one that burned down?"

"Yes." The memories of her late father's subsequent slide into depression brought Belinda's thoughts full circle. "The doctors said he died from a heart attack but I think he just gave up caring about anything, even his own life, after he lost the church." She hardened her heart. "Getting back to Paul Randall. I don't care where he stays or what he does while he's here as long as I don't have to deal with him. I'll be delighted if I never lay eyes on him again."

"You sound like you really mean that."

"I've never meant anything more in my whole life."

Paul managed to keep himself occupied all afternoon by strolling around town and stopping to make casual conversation whenever he got the opportunity. He was amazed at how few of the old-timers recognized him at first. And at how shocked they looked when he identified himself. Clearly, they remembered the punk kid with the perpetual chip on his shoulder and were having trouble believing the changes he'd made in his image. *Good,* he thought, satisfied. That was exactly what he'd intended.

Beginning at the Mom and Pop café and gas station located next to the only traffic light in town, he worked his way through the pharmacy and the farm bureau office, then strolled the last block to the town square. A green, close-cropped lawn surrounded the courthouse. Most of the benches in the shade of the maple trees were occupied by old men, heads nodding sleepily. As usual, Serenity was so serene it gave him the willies.

Paul snorted in self-derision as he entered the hardware store on the north side of the square. All the businesses on that block faced the old brick courthouse, which meant he could stand on the opposite side of the square and position himself to look directly at the door to the Chamber of Commerce without attracting undue attention.

Ever since he'd learned Belinda worked there, he'd been trying to ignore that particular office. And he'd failed miserably. It looked like he was either going to have to pay his old flame a visit and try to clear the air, or resign himself to his grinding gut and buy a giant supply of antacids to calm the ulcer that usually flared up when he was under a lot of stress.

Paul opted for the visit. He'd written dozens of letters to Belinda over the years but had never mailed any of them. Initially, he'd focused on defending himself until he'd realized how futile that was. Later, he'd simply apologized for his anger. The last attempt had been a letter of condolence when he'd heard that her father had died. Worried that it might seem inappropriate because of his volatile past association with the man, he'd torn it up instead of sending it.

Remembering, he paused near the front of the hardware store, just inside the door.

"Something I can help you with, mister?" the skinny, slightly stooped proprietor asked. "You'd best hurry. We're about to close."

Paul snapped out of his reverie and smiled pleasantly. "Sorry. I was just looking, anyway. Do you happen to know how late the Chamber of Commerce stays open?"

"Till five, like the rest of us," the man said. "Why?"

"Just wondered."

"You're not from around here, are you?"

Chuckling, Paul shook his head. That was at least the tenth time that day he'd been asked the same question in exactly the same words. "Nope. I'm an outsider. Definitely an outsider." He offered his hand. "The name's Randall. The Whitaker sisters are my great-aunts."

Accepting Paul's hand, the proprietor shook it

heartily. "Well, well. I didn't know Miss Prudence and Miss Patience had kin in these parts. Where'd you say you was from?"

"I settled in Harrison after I got out of law school," Paul told him. "I'm just visiting here."

"Well, if you're fixin' to repair that old house of theirs, we got the best selection of plumbing and electrical parts in the county."

"I'll keep that in mind. Thanks for your time." When the man opened his mouth and began to add to his sales pitch, Paul headed for the door. "I can't stay and talk right now, but I'll be sure to check back with you later. I need to run over to the Chamber office before it closes."

"Tell Miss Belinda I said howdy."

"Right." Waving a congenial goodbye, Paul crossed the wide, shady street at an angle and started to jog across the courthouse lawn. The digital clock in front of the bank on the north-west corner read four fifty-five.

All afternoon Belinda had fidgeted at her desk, eagerly awaiting quitting time so she could close the office. She'd already straightened the racks of brochures and maps several times and dusted everything in sight. All that was left to do was turn off the lights, lock up and make a dash for home. The sooner the better.

At five minutes to five, she started for the door, the click of her heels echoing in the empty office.

Surely all the evenings she'd stayed open late would make up for leaving a few minutes early this time. One hand was poised over the Open sign, the other reaching for the lock, when a dark-haired, sophisticated-looking man in navy blue slacks and a sky-blue sport shirt appeared at the door.

He was tall, broad-shouldered and moved with an athletic grace. His hair was cut in the smooth, full style of a successful executive, except that it was long enough in the back to brush against his shirt collar.

Belinda's heart recognized him a few seconds before her brain agreed. She froze in mid-motion, sorely tempted to slam the door and bolt it. She didn't care if she did represent Serenity. That didn't mean she had to be nice to the likes of Paul Randall.

He glanced at his gleaming gold wristwatch. "I thought I still had a few minutes."

"Sorry. The office is closed."

"Too bad," he said with a wry smile. "I need some information about this interesting little town."

Belinda was not about to let him get the upper hand. "Fine." She grabbed a random handful of colorful brochures pertaining to the area and thrust them at him. "Here."

"I'm afraid that won't do," Paul said, stepping through the half-open door.

She gave ground. "I told you. The office is closed." The spicy aroma of his aftershave affected her strongly and made her want to put even more distance between them.

Paul's smile grew into a self-satisfied grin as he looked her up and down. "Humor me. I have as much right as anybody to be treated with respect. All I want from you is a few facts."

Whether she liked it or not, he'd made a good point. Fair was fair. Besides, it wouldn't do to let on that she was still mad enough at him to make her blood boil. A contrary man like Paul Randall would probably enjoy seeing that she was upset, and she wasn't going to give him that satisfaction.

Circling him widely, hurriedly, Belinda said, "All right. What can the Serenity Chamber of Commerce do for you? I'll give you two minutes."

Paul's gaze met hers, challenged it, held it. "I'm good, but I'm not *that* good. Perhaps I'd better come back tomorrow when you have more free time."

And make me go through this emotional turmoil all over again? No way! The smartest thing she could do was give him the information he wanted, right now, and be rid of him.

"That won't be necessary," she said, pleased at how calm and businesslike she sounded in spite of her quaking insides and righteous indignation. She rounded the end of the counter to put a solid physical barrier between them. "What is it you need?"

"Well... A list of the commercial property within four blocks in any direction from my aunts' estate, for starters."

"You need to go to the county office for that and you know it," Belinda said, scowling. "What do you *really* want?"

Inwardly tense, Paul kept his posture relaxed, his smile as enigmatic as he could make it. He'd known that facing Belinda again would be difficult but he'd had no idea what a strong, gut-level reaction he'd have to her. That had been such a surprise he found he could hardly think straight, let alone come up with reasonable-sounding excuses for tracking her down while he was in town.

The most sensible option was probably to tell her the plain truth. The minute he'd set foot in Serenity again he'd felt he had to see her, to talk to her, to make her understand that he hadn't been responsible for the loss of her father's church. He was good at arguing court cases. It should have been easy to present a logical defense of his innocence.

Unfortunately, Paul had to admit he was currently standing on a foundation of emotional quicksand and sinking fast. Any notion he'd had about being permanently immune to Belinda's charms had vanished the moment he'd faced her again. If anything, the attraction he felt now was stronger than ever. That conclusion didn't astonish him nearly as much as the fact that the memory of her rejection still hurt.

If it hadn't been for her cautious expression and stiff, standoffish posture he might have foolishly relaxed his guard and told her how he felt, then and there. Which would have been the dumbest thing he'd done for ten years. Sharing some information about his professional concerns, however, didn't seem like such a bad idea. At least it would give him something intelligent to say.

"I was hoping you'd have time to bring me up to speed on the way Serenity is developing. You know. New business trends, population demographics, that kind of thing. Sort of an overview of what you see as the future of the town."

"Why me?"

"Because you've not only lived here for a long time, your job has put you right into the center of commerce." He quickly pressed on, hoping to sway her decision before she had a chance to think it through. "So, since you're about to close the office, how about I make reservations at Romano's for tonight? We can relax and talk over dinner."

"You've got to be kidding. No way!" Belinda's heart was racing and her mouth was as dry as the bottom of Lick Creek in mid-July! Didn't he remember anything about their last day together? About their quarrel? About the things she'd said to him? The passage of time had not changed her mind. Too many unanswered questions remained. Important questions. Questions she wasn't sure she wanted to ask because hearing the answers might prove too painful.

"Why not? Got a date with your doctor friend? I hear you two are quite a couple."

Obviously, Paul had been prying. "That's none of *your* business," she said stiffly.

"I see."

Belinda was surprised when he didn't immediately argue or try to manipulate her. As a practicing attorney he was obviously used to getting the results he wanted. Waiting for his counterattack, she pressed her lips into a thin line.

"Well, maybe some other time," Paul said, straightening and smiling woodenly. "I'll call you."

She noticed that his smile no longer brought a mischievous sparkle to his dark, compelling eyes. His gaze had grown shadowy, brooding, the way it used to be. The way it had been the night of the awful fire.

That memory was enough to keep her from holding back any longer. "No. I don't want you to call." Belinda shook her head firmly for emphasis. "We have nothing more to talk about."

Smile fading, he turned to leave. His voice sounded emotionless when he said, "For once, you may be right."

Belinda stopped by her grandmother Eloise's that evening. Eloise had sprained her ankle and was supposed to stay off her feet as much as possible. She wasn't behaving, of course. Belinda hadn't expected her to listen to medical advice, not even Sam's, which was why she'd decided to drop in and volunteer to cook the evening meal.

Standing at her grandmother's stove, Belinda got more and more distracted as she began to contrast the differences between Sam and Paul. Sam was steady, comfortable, and he fit effortlessly into her daily life. She'd never had a moment's worry about what he might be doing or who he might be with. On the other hand, being around Paul had always made her feel disquieted, as if she were standing at the edge of a precipice in a stiff wind and was about to be blown over the edge. Even now, though he'd looked as refined as any other professional man, his presence had sent a chill up her spine and made the hair on the back of her neck prickle.

Daydreaming, she nearly burned the black-eyed peas she was fixing as a side dish.

Eloise hobbled up to rescue the smoking pot and stirred rapidly. "Goodness me. That was close."

"Sorry. I guess I wasn't paying enough attention."

"No problem. I got to 'em in time." She paused, then asked, "So, tell me, how was Paul Randall?"

Whirling, Belinda stared. "How did you know I'd seen him?"

"Lucky guess." Eloise set the pot off to the side and plopped her slightly overweight body into a kitchen chair. "Well? Was he polite? Did he show his raisin', or did he manage to behave himself?"

"If you mean, did he grab me and kiss me sense- less the way he used to, the answer is no. He's more out-of-place in Serenity than ever, but he didn't say or do anything embarrassing.''

"That's a relief. You never know what might get back to Sam if somebody was to see you and Paul acting too friendly.''

"Don't be silly. I'm not even friends with Paul. Not anymore. Besides, Sam's not the jealous type. He may be practical to a fault but he's also predictable. He'd never jump to conclusions.'' Belinda turned off the stove and scooped thin strips of sautéed steak and onions from her frying pan into a serving bowl. "He's completely logical. That's why I believe him when he says Serenity's going to boom. He's even bought the building where his office is. Says he's planning to add another wing to it.''

"Well, well. I suppose that explains why he was so keen on being voted president of the Chamber. I'm not real happy to hear he wants to start changin' things, though.'' She lowered her voice to add, "'Course, he's not from around here, so you never know.''

Pensive, Belinda recalled what Paul had always said about not being accepted by the established core of Serenity's population. In his case, he was right. It wasn't that folks were cruel. Some newcomers just fit in better than others, especially if they made an effort to become a useful part of the community. Sam was making that effort. Paul and his father never had.

She remembered the first time she'd set eyes on Paul. His father had come to Serenity because of his late wife's shirttail relation to the Whitaker family and landed a job as a mechanic at the local gas station.

Paul had shown up for his first day as a senior at Serenity High sporting threadbare clothes, a worn leather jacket and a sullen, uncooperative attitude. Belinda had viewed him more as a lost soul than a rebel and had offered friendship. In no time, she'd fallen head-over-heels in love. She sighed. Too bad Paul's feelings for her hadn't been strong enough to overcome their differences.

"I'd like some of that before it gets cold," Eloise gibed, gesturing toward the bowl Belinda was holding. "Unless you plan on keepin' it all for yourself."

The comment brought her back to the present with a jolt. "Of course not. I…I was just afraid it was too hot for you to handle, that's all."

"Oh? With that faraway look in your eyes I figured you might be thinking about how you felt when you ran into your old boyfriend today." She grinned. "Was *he* too hot to handle, too?"

"Gram! Shame on you. Wash your mouth out!" Cheeks flaming, Belinda took her place at the table and refused to acknowledge her grandmother's triumphant expression. It was impossible to ignore her jubilant comments, however.

"Aha! I thought so. Good! Maybe now we'll see

some action around here. A little honest competition
should shake up Sam Barryman and get things moving. He may not be perfect but he's the best catch
around...and a doctor, to boot. You two have been
courtin' for a whole year. It's time he got serious
and asked you to marry him. Fish or cut bait, I always say.''

Belinda stared at her plate without seeing it. Sam
had already asked her to be his wife—more than
once—and she'd put him off. At the time, she hadn't
realized what was stopping her. Sam was personable
and reliable, he went to her church, and she was
truly fond of him. So why not make a commitment?
Why, indeed. Now that she'd been around Paul
again, she was beginning to understand that the
problem lay with her, not with Sam.

And she didn't like that conclusion one bit.

The Whitaker estate was a run-down relic from a
bygone era. It was also a prime piece of real estate,
which was why Paul had decided to spend a few
extra days poking around in Serenity. He knew his
elderly twin aunts had no spare funds with which to
have the place independently appraised. He also
knew that the sale of the property was their last
chance to provide for the fulfillment of any dreams
beyond day-to-day subsistence. At eighty-three, they
didn't have the option of going back to work teaching if they wanted anything more than the basic ne-
cessities.

He wheeled his black Lexus into the circular driveway of the old frame house and parked. The narrow track branched so that visitors who had arrived by carriage in the old days could enter by the front door, then send their driver to the back to stable the horses without having to turn the team around. The carriage house in the rear had eventually been converted into a garage.

Pausing in the quiet of the late evening, Paul gripped the steering wheel and took a deep, settling breath. Maybe he'd made a mistake by coming here. Even Aunt Patience, usually the sprightly, happy twin, had been acting reserved. Prudence, on the other hand, had always moped around as if she'd just lost her best friend, so he couldn't tell if she was glad he'd responded to her request for legal help or not.

But that wasn't his real reason for questioning the wisdom of his decision to visit Serenity, was it? He immediately pictured Belinda. They'd had some really good times together. On her eighteenth birthday she'd snuck away to spend the afternoon at the river with him. Her auburn hair was longer back then, with golden highlights glistening in the sun, and she'd pinned it up because the weather was so hot and sticky.

They'd walked beside the slow-flowing water, pausing in the shade to share a tender kiss. Paul remembered her wide, innocent, blue eyes looking at him as if he were the perfect man. Faint freckles had dotted her pale skin.

She'd wrinkled her nose and made a silly face, pleading with him. "Come on. It's just a picnic. Please? Promise you'll go with me?"

"A *church* picnic," Paul had said.

"So? Daddy won't bite."

"I'm not so sure. He didn't look real pleased when I sat down next to you last Sunday."

She giggled. "I know. Wasn't he funny? It was like he preached his whole sermon right to you."

"Yeah. I noticed." Paul grimaced. "I felt like a bug under a microscope."

Belinda slipped her arms around his waist and stepped into his embrace. "I'm so sorry. That was partly my fault. When Daddy asked me why I was spending so much time with you, I told him I was trying to get you converted."

"I don't need saving," Paul recalled telling her. Back then, he'd seriously considered walking the aisle some Sunday just to please her and make points with her father. Fortunately, he'd decided there was no way he could fake salvation, any more than he could convince the sanctimonious residents of Serenity that he was just as good as they were.

Pensive, he sighed. Funny how things had worked out. His father had ruined his own life by making lousy choices, had left the stigma of a convicted arsonist on his only son and had seen to it that they stayed ostracized by living a transient, antisocial life.

Yet it was that same miserable existence that had made Paul so determined to succeed, to earn enough money to change his lifestyle and make himself into someone entirely different. A professional man people could look up to. Respect.

And that strategy had worked until he'd faced Belinda Carnes again and sensed her continuing distrust. He'd hoped she'd give him some sign that she might be willing to forgive and forget. Maybe even take up where they'd left off. After her clear rebuff today, however, he knew better.

Innocent until proven guilty didn't apply to him. Not in Serenity. Belinda obviously still blamed him for setting fire to her father's church. Chances were, so did almost everybody else in town, even if they didn't have the guts to say so to his face.

Paul's jaw muscles tightened, and his forehead furrowed. He didn't care what the others thought of him, but Belinda's opinion mattered. A lot. Whether they ever got back together or not, it was imperative that he prove to her he'd been innocent of any wrongdoing.

He sure wished he knew how he was going to do that.

Chapter Two

Belinda smiled and waved when she saw Sam Barryman's sporty red Camaro pulling into her driveway at precisely nine-thirty on Sunday morning. It was hard to remember exactly when Sam had started taking her to church. He hadn't asked. He'd simply begun showing up. For the past six or eight months she'd accepted his presence without question. This morning, however, she found it strangely annoying.

Tall, blond and athletic, the doctor bounded up the front steps to her house and held the door open for her. "Good. You're on time. I'm glad to see my suggestions worked."

"I beg your pardon?" Belinda wrinkled her brow.

"My suggestions. About getting you organized," he said, ignoring her negative expression. "Can't have my future wife running around being late all the time."

Belinda couldn't decide which assumption she wanted to object to first. Having spent the past few days soul-searching, she decided on the farthest-reaching one. "I told you, Sam. We're good friends. There's no reason to spoil a great relationship by getting married."

"So you say." He slipped his arm around her waist and escorted her down the porch steps, not letting go until they reached his car. As he opened the passenger door for her he said, "If you weren't such a prude we could be having a lot more fun right now, though."

Belinda rolled her eyes. "We've been over and over this subject, Sam. It's not open to discussion."

Chuckling, he circled the car and slid behind the wheel. "Okay. But I'm not going to wait for you forever."

"I've never asked you to wait for me at all. That was your idea."

"Because you're worth it." He flashed her a toothpaste smile and reached over to pat her hand as he drove. "All I have to do is figure out how to make you wake up and realize I'd be the perfect husband for you."

Belinda wanted to refute his claim but something held her back. Was it possible Sam was right? Could she be making a terrible mistake? It was conceivable. Sam was a nice enough person, and according to her late father she'd never shown good judgment where men were concerned.

Lost in thought she smoothed the skirt of her silky teal blue dress, admiring the beautiful fabric. The dress was one of her favorites, even though Sam had admitted he didn't care for it. He preferred she wear tailored outfits in more subdued colors, especially when she accompanied him to Chamber dinners or other business functions. She didn't really mind.

When it came to attending church, however, she wanted to feel uplifted, joyful. Bright colors helped her do that. So did singing. When the organ, piano and choir voices filled the sanctuary with heavenly music, she was transported to a time of carefree childhood, when her family had been intact and she hadn't imagined she'd one day feel so alone. So abandoned. So...

Oh, stop! Belinda ordered in disgust. *You're being ridiculous. You have much more to be thankful for than a lot of people do. You should be ashamed of yourself.*

She truly was ashamed. After all, she still had Eloise and a whole church-full of dear friends, not to mention the other people in Serenity who cared about her. It was a wonderful place. Even with its small town politics and petty rivalries it beat living in a big city, where most neighbors didn't even know each other's names. Or care to learn them.

Sam's voice jarred her reverie as he wheeled the Camaro into the church parking lot. "Well, we're here. What are you thinking about? You looked awfully serious just now."

"Serenity," Belinda said, smiling. "The town, not the frame of mind. Sometimes I can hardly believe how perfect this place is."

"Hold that thought," he teased. "It's excellent PR for the Chamber of Commerce."

"I know." She looped her purse strap over one arm, cradled her Bible and got out. "Remember that the next time I ask for a raise."

"I will." As they started for the large, redbrick church he offered her his arm, waited until she took it, then leaned closer to add, "Of course, if you were my wife, you wouldn't have to worry about working."

Belinda decided it was wisest to treat his comment lightly. She batted her lashes, gazed at him melodramatically and said, "Oh, sugar pie, you mean I'd get to stay home with all twelve of our kids?"

Sam's resulting chuckle sounded more like choking than laughing. "How about we start with one or two?" He raised an eyebrow. "Or were you kidding?"

Stifling a giggle she told him, "I was kidding. I can't believe you thought I was serious."

"I never know with you. Your moods can be really hard to read sometimes."

"Oh?" Belinda was about to ask for clarification when she felt a tingle at the nape of her neck. She shivered. Looked back. A dignified man wearing dark glasses and driving a shiny black Lexus was

pulling into the parking lot. She didn't have to stare
to know it was Paul Randall.

Her ire rose. How *dare* he follow her to church!

Inside the sanctuary, Belinda tried to forget who
she'd seen arriving. She and Sam were seated in the
third row, as usual. Since she couldn't see Paul in
front of her, she assumed he had to be somewhere
behind. Was he far away? Close by? If she peeked
over her shoulder, would she spot him? Catch him
watching her so she could give him an appropriately
disapproving look in return? The thought of meeting
his intense gaze sent a frisson of electricity zinging
up her spine.

The congregation stood for the first hymn. Sam
offered to share his hymnbook, but Belinda didn't
need it. She'd memorized the words to most of the
songs as a child because if her father's church door
had been open, she and her mother were expected
to be there. Truth to tell, she hadn't concentrated on
her father's sermons nearly as well as she should
have. The beautiful, inspiring music, however, had
always captured and held her attention.

"Blessed assurance..." Voice clear and sweet,
she sang the first few words, then suddenly quieted.
Directly behind her an accomplished baritone was
harmonizing with so much feeling and skill it took
her breath away. He sounded familiar. Acting on
impulse, she glanced over her shoulder, certain she

had to be mistaken. She wasn't. Paul Randall was standing in the next row back, singing his heart out!

"...of glory divine..." Sam elbowed her and thrust the open hymnal at her again. Hands trembling, Belinda grasped one side of it and stared at the printed page. Looking at the words didn't help a bit. Her mind was whirling so fast she couldn't focus. All she could do was listen in awe.

It was like a miracle! Paul sounded as if he really meant what the song was saying. Whenever she'd managed to drag him into church as a teen he'd acted so sullen he hadn't even opened his mouth, let alone shown any musical talent. What a magnificent voice he had! She could listen to singing like that all day and never tire of it.

The hymn ended. Belinda followed Sam's lead and quietly sat down, but her spirit was still soaring. Paul's voice had touched every nerve in her body, echoed from the corners of her heart and lifted her soul to a higher plane.

What a shame he isn't in the choir, she thought absently. Logic immediately contradicted the notion. *Bad idea.* It would strain her already tenuous emotions if she had to see Paul sitting with the other members of the choir every Sunday. Good thing he didn't actually live around here! Imagining him as an active member of her church was probably nothing more than emotional regression, she reasoned, wishful thinking left over from her youth.

Taking a shaky breath, Belinda decided that was

exactly what was happening. At eighteen, she'd hoped and prayed that Paul would join her father's church, settle down and become a productive member of the community, someone she could introduce to everyone, including her dad, without feeling she had to make excuses.

Now, all that had changed. She had matured. Her father had died. Whether or not Paul Randall had truly bettered himself was no longer her concern. If he hadn't returned to Serenity she might never even have thought of him again.

Her conscience immediately disagreed, forming a stern but silent, *Ha!* Focusing on the stained-glass window behind the preacher, she escaped into silent prayer.

Oh, Father, forgive me. You've blessed me so much. Why can't I be satisfied and thankful and not want things that are bad for me? Sighing, she added, *Things like Paul Randall.*

As if the timing were preordained, the congregation began to sing a second hymn. There was no way Belinda could fight the emotional impact that Paul's impressive voice had on her, so she gave up trying. Closing her eyes, she drank in the deep vibrations the way the thirsty Ozark hills soaked up the first spring rains.

When she finally opened her eyes, Sam was staring at her as if she'd just committed an unpardonable sin.

In a way, she agreed with him.

* * *

Paul decided to linger in the parking lot outside the church and lay in wait for Belinda and Sam after the service concluded. When he'd chosen a seat behind them he'd convinced himself he was only doing it to force Belinda to introduce him to Sam. That was partially true. He did want to meet the doctor for the first time on a social level so he could size him up better.

What Paul hadn't anticipated, however, was how being so close to Belinda for a whole hour would affect him. Or how his thoughts would wander and his perception intensify whenever he looked her way.

He noticed she was wearing her hair shorter these days. It lay smoother and curved under gently, just touching her shoulders, with the sides tucked behind her ears. Delicate pearl earrings reflected the shimmering blue of her dress. The color was like sunlight reflecting on rippling water. It reminded him of the summer days they'd walked along the banks of the Strawberry River, holding hands and stealing kisses. At that time, he'd assumed they were simply seeking privacy, which was just fine with him. The more chances he could get to kiss her, to hold her, the better. In retrospect, he supposed Belinda had wanted to go to private places like that because she'd been ashamed to be seen in public with him.

And speaking of public, Paul mused, she and her boyfriend had just come out of the church and were headed his way. He purposely stepped forward to block their path. When Belinda looked at him their eyes met. Held. Paul called upon his battle-seasoned courtroom smile. "Good morning, Ms. Carnes."

Cheeks reddening, she mumbled, "Good morning."

He continued to smile amiably. "Aren't you going to introduce me to your friend?"

Why not? Maybe then Paul would believe she and Sam were a steady couple and leave her alone, like she'd asked. Belinda managed to tear her gaze from Paul's long enough to look over her shoulder at Sam. "Dr. Sam Barryman, Paul Randall."

Paul was the first to reach out. "Pleased to meet you." He wondered for a long moment if the doctor was going to refuse to shake his hand.

"Same here," Sam finally said, grasping his hand firmly, briefly. "You're that lawyer, aren't you? I'd heard you were in town."

Paul chuckled. "I imagine everybody has. Word travels pretty fast around here. Actually, I came to advise my aunts on the sale of their property." Striking a deliberately casual pose, he shrugged. "But I guess you know that, too." When Sam didn't comment, he went on. "Folks tell me you've managed to make a place for yourself in Serenity. That's not an easy thing to do. Congratulations."

"Thanks." Sam slid his arm around Belinda's waist and urged her away. "Well, nice to have met you, Randall."

"Same here." A cynical smile lifted one corner of Paul's mouth. Now that he'd met the doctor, he had the advantage, which was how he liked it. Sam Barryman was a smooth operator. Everything about him looked good—his professional demeanor, his expensive suit, his perfectly styled hair…the home-town girl he was courting. But something about him wasn't quite right. When Paul had looked into his eyes he'd seen a brief flash of wariness that didn't belong there, assuming the man was as honest as his reputation implied.

Thoughtful, Paul watched him hurry Belinda away. For a guy who had nothing to hide, good old Sam sure was in a rush to leave. Maybe it was time to press him a little harder and see how he reacted. He started after the retreating couple.

Belinda disengaged herself from Sam's posses-sive grasp as they approached his car. "What's the matter with you?"

"I don't know what you're talking about."

She saw him glance toward the church, so she did the same. Her heart skipped a beat. Paul was rapidly following them! Could Sam be getting jealous, just like Gramma Eloise had predicted? It sure seemed like it. And by the way, where *was* Eloise? She rarely missed a Sunday service.

Paul slowed as he approached. "Whew. I didn't realize how muggy it was out here." He shed his suit jacket and loosened his tie as he smiled at Belinda. "I meant to tell you, that dress looks great on you. It reminds me of summer days like today."

Since Sam was standing so close, it was easier to relax and casually accept the compliment. "Thanks. It's a favorite of mine."

"I can see why."

Behind her, Sam opened the car door. "Belinda?"

"Sorry," Paul said quickly. "Don't let me keep you. We can always arrange a time to get together later and talk."

Belinda couldn't believe his arrogance! She'd innocently acknowledged one comment about her dress and he immediately assumed that was all it took to win her over. What conceit! She stiffened defensively. "I told you before, Paul. I don't think you and I should have anything more to do with each other."

He nodded. "I'm afraid you misunderstood me. I meant that Dr. Barryman and I needed to have a private talk. I suppose it is inevitable that I'll bump into you again, though. This is a pretty small town." The corners of his mouth lifted in a smug-looking smile. "Tell you what. I promise to do everything I can to avoid you. How's that sound?"

"Wonderful." Feeling like an idiot, Belinda shaded her eyes and focused her attention on Sam. "Okay. What's going on here? Why does Paul want to talk to you in private? I'm starting to feel like

I've come in halfway through a complicated movie and can't make sense out of the plot."

She saw the doctor set his jaw stubbornly, so she turned back to Paul. "Well? I'm waiting. Which one of you is going to fill me in?"

"I have no objection," Paul said, maintaining his casual air. "It has to do with the sale of the Whitaker estate."

"Why do you need to talk to Sam about that?"

"Because your boyfriend, here, is up to his eyeballs in the deal. I'm surprised he didn't tell you."

Frowning, Belinda said, "So am I." It was bad enough that Sam was keeping an important secret from her. To learn about it from smug, gloating Paul Randall was much worse.

At that moment, if someone had asked her to choose which of the two men was more irritating, she'd have been hard-pressed to decide.

By the time Sam dropped her off at home, Belinda had managed to find out very little about his plans. All he'd say was that he had some wealthy silent partners whose interests he needed to protect, and that what he was trying to accomplish would be good for Serenity. She'd been around him long enough to know he couldn't be badgered into revealing more details until he was ready.

Since he hadn't offered to take her out for Sunday dinner the way he usually did, she assumed he was miffed. Well, too bad. If he expected her to ever consider him husband material, he was going to have to accept the fact that she expected to be treated as an equal partner in any serious relationship.

She opened the passenger door and stepped out as soon as Sam stopped his car in her driveway. "Thanks for the ride."

He leaned across the seat. "Belinda?"

Pausing, she bent down to see what he wanted.

"Is it true?" he asked.

"Is what true?"

"You and Randall. I'd heard a few rumors but I didn't pay much attention to them. I figured you'd never go for a guy like that. I mean, his father was a bum with a prison record, wasn't he?"

Belinda's stomach tightened, though not from hunger. "Paul's father was an auto mechanic when we met. What the man may have done before he and Paul moved to Serenity is none of my business." *Or yours.*

"And they lived in a shack out behind Butch's gas station where the old man worked?"

"It was a trailer, not a shack," she answered. "It was the best poor Mr. Randall could do, under the circumstances. Paul worked odd jobs to help out...." She paused, then added, "Until he went away to college."

"I've heard all about the night he left," Sam said, "but I won't go into that because I don't want to bring up memories that are painful for you."

Oh, right, Belinda thought. *As if you haven't already.* "Why are you asking me so much about Paul?"

"I've found it pays to know my enemies."

"Paul's not your enemy. Besides, there's absolutely nothing between us. Not anymore."

Sam began to smile at her. "I know that, honey. I just wanted to see if you were in a good position to help me out. I think you are."

"Help you? How?"

"I need to find out what Randall's plans are for the Whitaker place and how close we are to coming to terms during negotiations." His grin grew. "If you and I work together, we'll have a definite advantage."

Belinda refused to believe he was asking her to become some kind of amateur spy. Sam would never do that. He might be overly practical but he wasn't nefarious.

"What I have in mind is for the good of Serenity," Sam added. "I promise. You'll see. The whole town will benefit."

"From *what?*"

Chuckling, Sam straightened, making her bend lower to look him in the eye. "Oh, no, you don't. I'll let you in on my plan when the time comes. Until then, it's my little secret. All you have to do is be your charming self and report whatever Randall tells you about my project."

"Didn't you hear what I said to Paul this morning? I never intend to see him again, let alone talk to him.''

Sam looked triumphant. ''On the contrary. You're going to see Randall this coming Wednesday night.''

''I am? How? Where?'' Her heart began to pound at the thought. The sticky afternoon air no longer seemed to contain enough oxygen, no matter how rapidly she breathed.

''At the business dinner I told you about last week. We'll be representing the Chamber, remember?''

''Yes, but...''

''I guess I forgot to mention that it's at the Whitaker house. That location wouldn't have been my choice, but we'll make the best of it. Now that I've seen what kind of man Randall is, I'm certain he'll be there.'' He paused and slipped the car into gear. ''I know he said he liked that dress, but wear that simple black dress of yours instead, so he keeps his mind on the deal, will you? I'll pick you up Wednesday at six-thirty sharp.''

As Belinda watched him drive away, she was surprised how aggravated she was. Sam's attitude made her feel like blurting out a few colorful phrases that had never before passed her lips. She wouldn't do it, of course. It was wrong to curse, even if what she said didn't actually take the Lord's name in vain.

But after the morning she'd just had, she certainly understood what drove people to say such things!

Boy, did she.

Chapter Three

Restless, Belinda immediately changed from the teal dress to shorts and a loose shirt, then walked over to her grandmother's house rather than phoning to see why she hadn't been in church that morning. Eloise had ventured into the garden in spite of her sore ankle and was carefully watering a bed of new seedlings. She smiled a greeting.

Belinda pushed her bangs off her forehead. "Whew. I can see why you're out here watering. It's sure hot today."

"No kidding."

"So, what's new? How come you missed church?"

"I didn't miss it." Eloise shot her a brief glance, then squeezed the trigger of the sprayer again and went back to watching the spritzing water.

"You were there this morning? I didn't see you."

"I sat way in the back with Verleen and Miss Mercy. We get a much better view of all the goings-on from there. And now that the church has those hearing assistance doodads, we don't have to be so close to the front to keep from missing the important stuff."

Eyes twinkling, Belinda gibed, "You three never miss a thing, and you know it. I'm surprised you don't sit up in the sound booth and train binoculars on the rest of the congregation through that little window."

"Ooh, good idea!"

"I thought you'd like it."

Eloise waited a moment, then said, "So, tell me all about your morning."

"It was interesting, to say the least." Belinda blew a noisy breath. "Paul Randall showed up in church, but I'm sure you know that already. I don't understand why he didn't just go to services with his aunts."

"And have to choose whether to go to Patience's big, fancy church over in East Serenity, or Pru's little one? That's a no-win situation. The boy's not crazy."

"He's also not a boy anymore." She pulled a face. "You were right about Sam getting jealous of him."

"Aha! I knew it. Wonderful!"

"Not exactly," Belinda said cynically. "I don't

think I like Sam as well when he's acting so possessive."

"Nonsense. That's a man's way of showing you he cares. They're not very good at putting it into words, you know."

Belinda shook her head. "No, I *don't* know. Dad was always hugging Mom and telling her he loved her. He used to hug people in his congregation, too. I don't remember him doing it much after Mom died, though." She hesitated, then decided to go on. "At home, he acted like he was mad at me all the time. I would have given anything to get one of his big bear hugs in those days."

"Oh, honey..." Eloise laid aside the sprayer and enfolded her in a motherly embrace. "Your daddy didn't mean anything by it. He was just hurting and afraid."

"Afraid?" She stepped back to study her grandmother's expression. "Of what? He was always preaching about the strength we should draw from our Christian faith. How could he have been afraid?"

"Because he was human. Preachers are, you know. I think he pulled away from everybody because he couldn't bear to be hurt again." She caressed Belinda's cheek. "He loved you very, very much. That was why he acted so strict about everything. He was just trying to protect you."

Sniffling, Belinda made a wry face. "Well, it worked. I'm probably the only twenty-seven-year-old virgin in Serenity...or in the world, for that matter." The rosy color rising on Eloise's cheeks made her laugh.

The older woman giggled, too. "I don't know how you've managed to avoid getting carried away." The pink in her cheeks darkened, and her eyes were bright. "I was a very respectable girl, but I'm not sure I could have resisted your grandpa much longer than I did. We were too much in love to want to wait."

Belinda sighed, shrugged. "I suppose that's the key. Love, I mean. Sam says I'm a prude. He's right."

"You haven't been tempted?"

"Some," Belinda admitted. "But we always managed to stop before it was too late."

"Was Sam upset? Men have very fragile egos, you know."

With a smirk and a quick shake of her head, Belinda looked bravely into Eloise's eyes. "Sam didn't have a thing to do with it," she said. "He wasn't the man I was with when it happened."

Belinda would never forget the night she and Paul had almost stepped across the line. The balmy spring evening was so lovely it was as if it had been made especially for lovers. For them. She'd ridden close behind him on his motorcycle, reveling in the perfect opportunity to wrap her arms around his waist and lay her cheek against his back.

Paul had pulled over just outside Sylamore, on a

bluff overlooking the river. Reluctantly, she'd released her hold on him and they'd strolled hand in hand toward an immense, flat-topped boulder at the edge of the scenic-view parking area.

Sighing, she'd said, "Look how clear the sky is. You can even see the Milky Way tonight."

He'd drawn her into his embrace then, and kissed her soundly, passionately. "All I want to look at is you."

Weak in the knees, she'd slipped her arms around his neck and held tight. "Oh, Paul. I love you so much."

"I love you, too, Belinda. I just wish..."

"What?" she whispered against his lips.

"Let's go sit down." Paul led her to the boulder, climbed it and reached to pull her up beside him. He took off his leather jacket and spread it out. "Here. Sit on this so you don't get your clothes all dirty."

So filled with happiness she thought she'd burst, Belinda did as he asked and snuggled as close to him as she could get. She'd just begun to imagine what it would be like to spend the rest of her life in Paul's arms when he said, "I may be going away soon."

That was unthinkable! "No!" Throwing herself at him, Belinda held on as if he were bidding her a final goodbye that very night. "You can't leave. You can't. Please don't go!" Frantic, she threaded her fingers through his long, thick hair and began raining kisses over his face, his neck, his chest.

Paul had managed to keep his youthful urges pretty much under control until that moment. She heard him moan and felt his hands start to rove over her back, then come up under her arms to touch her where no one else ever had.

"Run away with me," Paul begged, an emotional catch in his voice. "Marry me, Belinda. Marry me."

She'd almost said yes to more than marriage that night. Breathing hard, her heart pounding, she'd fought her own desires until the immense effort had brought tears to her eyes. One kiss, one forbidden touch, had led to another and another and another.

That was when she'd opened her eyes, looked at the canopy of stars, recognized God's magnificent handiwork and been reminded of her vow to her Heavenly Father. Somehow, she'd mustered the strength of will to push Paul away in spite of his protests.

To this day, she didn't know how she'd talked herself into it.

Paul spent the next two days shuttling between Serenity and his office in Harrison, checking tax records and trying to find out if Sam Barryman had the financial backing he claimed. By late Tuesday afternoon he was back in Serenity, waiting for his secretary to call with more information. He poured himself a tall glass of the lemonade his aunts had made and took it out to their front porch.

Prattling, Patience trailed him. "Can you believe it? She went shopping and was so late for her hair appointment she had to go straight to Angela's!"

"Who? Aunt Prudence?" He tipped the frosted glass and drank half its tangy contents.

"Of course. Who else is the bane of my existence? I made her the appointment because I wanted us both to look decent for tomorrow night. Oh, the lovely parties our family used to host in this very house. And now we'll get to do it again, right here, one last time."

"It's not exactly a party," Paul reminded her. "It's a business dinner."

Patience flipped a hand in the air, bracelets jingling. "Oh, who cares. We're entertaining. That's all that matters to me. You're such a sweetheart to offer to pay for it all." She patted his arm and smiled wistfully. "I can't wait to get my money out of this old place and take off on a world cruise."

"It might be best to invest the profits and use the interest instead of dipping into the principle."

"Oh, pooh," Patience said. "My sister can stick around here and sulk away her life if she wants to. I'm going to get out and have some fun." She smoothed her cap of silver hair. "Which reminds me. Since Prudence has our station wagon, can you give me a lift to the beauty salon?"

Paul checked his watch. "In another half hour or

so. I'm waiting for an important call. I told my secretary I could be reached at your number.''

"Oh! Oh, dear. I'm afraid that won't do. I have to be there in fifteen minutes,'' she said, casting him a bright grin. "I have an idea. I can borrow *your* car.''

Paul nearly strangled on his lemonade. "My new Lexus?''

"Yes! I've always wanted to drive a beautiful car like that. It'll be the thrill of my life.'' Displaying a pitiful expression she said, "I don't have a lot of time left to collect great experiences like that, you know.''

What could he say when she put it that way? Patience's reflexes still seemed keen enough to cope with a short trip across town. She was quick-witted and sprightly, which made her seem more youthful than her twin, even though Prudence always stressed that she was eleven minutes younger.

Sighing in resignation, he reached into his pocket and held out his keys. "Promise you'll be careful?''

She drew an imaginary X across her chest with a long, lacquered fingernail. "I promise. Now be a dear and back it out for me, will you? I have trouble judging distances in those fancy mirrors.''

"How do you know you do?''

Patience giggled behind her hand. "I'm afraid I've been naughty. I've been sitting in your lovely black car and pretending to drive it.'' She clapped her hands. "This time, I won't have to pretend!''

Paul rolled his eyes and sighed. Great-Aunt Patience certainly knew how to get whatever she wanted. In her prime, she must have been a real femme fatale. He couldn't help wondering why she and her twin had turned out so differently.

"Prudence tells me Patience is having the whole affair catered," Eloise informed Belinda when she stopped by after work the following Tuesday. "All except for my special carrot cake. Pru wanted me to make one as a surprise."

"Great. If dinner's no good, I'll just wait for dessert and fill up on your delicious cake."

Grinning broadly, Eloise got up and started for the kitchen. She was limping noticeably. Belinda frowned. "How's your ankle?"

"Fine. It hardly bothers me at all if I stay off it. Just makes me mad is all. I'd like it better if I didn't have to act my age."

"Sixty-five isn't old," Belinda argued. "What if you were in your eighties like the Whitaker twins? Besides, since when did you act your age?"

Eloise laughed. "Probably never. I suppose that's what keeps me feeling so young. At least most of the time." Wincing, she plopped down in a kitchen chair and pointed to the refrigerator. "I've got to sit a spell. The cake's in there. Take a peek."

Opening the refrigerator door, Belinda immediately spotted the lavish dessert and lifted it out with great care. "Oh, it's beautiful! You really outdid yourself this time."

"I wanted it to be extra nice so I used slivered almonds and made a sweet cream cheese icing. Putting it on that footed glass plate dresses it up a lot, too." She carefully propped her ankle on the chair next to her. "So, can you deliver it for me?"

"Me?" Belinda's heart did a back flip and landed in a lump in her throat. "When?"

"Well, I suppose you could take it with you when you and Sam go to dinner at the Whitakers', but it would be much better if it was already there when the caterers arrive. That way, we can be sure Pru won't be disappointed."

Reflecting upon the time of day and the fact that the spinster sisters would undoubtedly be home, Belinda got control of her vivid imagination and forced herself to calm down. Paul had kept his promise to avoid her. She hadn't seen him since Sunday morning. There was no reason to assume he'd be at his aunts'. And even if he was, so what? The problem wasn't Paul, it was *her*.

"Okay," Belinda said with a nod. "I can drop it by on my way to the city council meeting."

"Uh-oh. I forgot this was Tuesday. No wonder you didn't change your clothes after work. Never mind, dear. I'll take it myself."

"No, you won't. You'll stay right where you are and rest that ankle. Is there anything else you need before I leave?"

"No. I'm fine. I'll have a pizza delivered for supper. Stop by after the meeting if you like and we can share the leftovers."

Belinda chuckled. "Are you sure? The way those meetings drag on it could be midnight before I'm free."

"I don't mind a late visit as long as it's you," Eloise said fondly.

Carefully balancing the cake, Belinda leaned sideways to kiss her grandmother on the cheek. "Wow. Love and pizza. An unbeatable combination. I have the perfect life."

"I think you'll find there's a little more to a perfect life than that."

"Oh, I hope not." Belinda made the exchange into a silly joke to keep from taking herself too seriously. "I was just getting the pepperoni part figured out."

Belinda parked her white Tercel on the tree-lined street in front of the Whitaker house, immensely relieved to see that there was no black Lexus in the narrow driveway. She closed her eyes and whispered, "Thank you, God."

Not that she was scared of running into Paul. She just saw no reason to face him again unless she was forced to. Clearly, the Lord agreed, because the man was gone.

Balancing the heavy glass cake plate, Belinda detoured around an overgrown cedar and made her way along the side of the dilapidated old house. A fat yellow cat sat in the middle of the back porch, licking its paw to wash its face and regally ignoring her presence.

Belinda didn't want to put the cake down or balance it in one hand to knock on the kitchen door so she called through the screen. "Miss Prudence? I brought your cake."

No one answered. By nudging the bottom of the warped wooden frame with the toe of her shoe, she was able to pry the screen door open and duck through safely before it banged shut behind her. Except for the tabby cat roosting on top of the refrigerator and the black-and-white kittens playing with a catnip mouse under the table, the house seemed deserted.

"Oh, well. No problem," Belinda told herself, easily deciding what to do. She'd just tuck the cake into the refrigerator where it belonged and be on her way. That would preserve the freshness of the cream cheese icing and also keep the house cats from helping themselves to a taste after she left.

She yanked open the refrigerator door. Her jaw dropped. So did a package of wilted lettuce and a roll of premade biscuits. The cardboard cylinder around the biscuits popped open as it hit the floor. Startled, Belinda almost made the terrible mistake of jeopardizing the cake in her efforts to stem the avalanche.

At her feet, biscuit dough was slowly expanding

through the break in the package. One of the black-and-white kittens was sneaking up on it as if it were dangerous prey. Looking from the crammed refrigerator shelves to the large, footed glass plate, Belinda muttered, "What in the world am I going to do with *this?*"

Her gaze centered on the odd bowls and half-empty packages of food she could see near the front of the shelves. Could she ever clear a big enough place? Maybe. In an hour or so. Give or take a day.

One thing was certain. She was going to be late for the council meeting.

Paul was upstairs, on the phone to his secretary, when he thought he heard the back door slam. Relieved, he assumed Patience had finally brought his car home.

As soon as he finished his conversation he started downstairs to give her a chance to tell him about the fun she'd had with his poor Lexus. It was insured, of course, but that didn't mean he'd welcome a dented fender. Or a dented great-aunt!

His running shoes made little sound on the carpet. It wasn't until he was almost to the kitchen that he heard the soft singing of a woman. That wasn't Patience. Or Prudence. It sounded like... Belinda?

Slowing his pace, Paul approached with caution. After her insistence that she didn't want to see or talk to him, Belinda couldn't possibly be there. It had to be a trick of his imagination. Or a singing burglar with a high, sweet voice, he countered, purposely mocking himself.

He reached the doorway. There was no need to look. Now that he was close enough to hear every word of her gospel song, he was certain his visitor was Belinda Carnes. But why? What was she up to? And why give herself away by making unnecessary noise?

Frowning, Paul leaned against the doorjamb, silently watching her. She was poking around in the refrigerator, a no-man's-land if he'd ever encountered one. Open bowls, cups and plates were stacked on the closest end of the counter. Wrapped packages of food were piled high on a chair she'd pulled over beside her and she was cautiously sniffing the contents of a large Mason jar, apparently checking them for freshness.

He waited until he thought she was about to step back, then calmly said, "Hello."

Belinda screeched, jumped and whirled around, all at the same time. The quart jar she'd been holding slipped out of her grasp. It hit the floor flat on its bottom, broke and spurted spaghetti sauce straight up in the air like a garlic-flavored geyser. What didn't get on her splattered all over the chair, cabinets and floor.

Heart pounding, she confronted Paul. "What did you do that for!"

"Me?" It was all he could do to keep from bursting into laughter. "I'm not the one who got caught raiding somebody else's refrigerator."

"I wasn't raiding it!"

"Oh? It looks to me like you were." He gestured toward the food she'd spread out. "What's all that?"

"It's..." Her anger increased when she saw the runny red splotches dotting everything, from the floor to the top of the counter and beyond. "A mess."

"That's true."

"This is not funny, Paul."

"Oh, I don't know." A broad grin was spread across his face. "It looks pretty funny from over here."

"Oh, yeah? Well, it doesn't from where I'm standing, and I'll thank you to butt out."

He shrugged nonchalantly. "Okay. If that's what you want. I suppose it won't hurt the floor much more if you walk over to the sink to get the paper towels yourself." With a chuckle he added, "You might want to slip your shoes off first, though. I hope they were red to start with."

"No. They were white," Belinda snapped, disgusted. "White linen. And new. I'll probably have to throw them away now."

"Not to mention chucking a lot of the stuff on the chair," he said, pointing.

"I can't do that. It's not mine." Worried, she surveyed the chaos, unsure where to begin.

"Well, I can," Paul said firmly. "I've been looking for a good excuse to dump a lot of those scraps before my aunts make the mistake of eating them and wind up with food poisoning. Wait there. I'll go get a big trash can from outside."

He returned almost immediately and set a black rubber trash can at the perimeter of the exploding sauce circle. "Here you go."

"Thanks." Belinda's conscience was really starting to bother her. She'd snapped at Paul and told him she didn't want to even talk to him, yet here he was, volunteering to help. "It's really nice of you to pitch in like this."

"I beg your pardon?" Arms folded across his chest, he stood back and stared at her.

She didn't like the shrewd look in his eyes or his posture of authority. "You were going to help me."

"I don't think I said that, exactly." The corners of his mouth lifted in a sly smile. "I believe I said I'd bring you a can. I did. I trust you to decide what's worth keeping and what should be tossed out." He raised one hand as if administering an oath. "I hereby promote you from refrigerator raider to garbage sorter. Go for it. Get busy. I'll just watch."

"Why you...you..." Belinda barely managed to squelch the desire to tell him off. There she stood, in her ruined shoes and dripping skirt, while he made stupid jokes at her expense. Him and his spotless shirt and perfectly creased jeans and detestable attitude of superiority. What Mr. Paul Randall needed was to be taken down a peg. And she was just the one to do it.

Struggling to keep her rising temper a secret, she said, "I don't want to track this mess all the way to the sink. Would you mind handing me the roll of paper towels?" It nearly choked her to add, "Please."

For a few long seconds it looked as if Paul wasn't going to comply. Finally, he turned and strolled to the sink and back. Sidestepping a splash next to the chair, he held the roll of towels out to her at arms' length.

Belinda couldn't quite reach it without moving her feet beyond the main sauce puddle. "You think you're standing far enough away?" she asked sarcastically. "I won't bite."

"Maybe not, but you sure are a mess." Paul chuckled heartily. "The stuffy Serenity Chamber of Commerce should see you now!"

If her conscience had ever possessed the slightest chance of stopping her, Paul's mocking, overbearing attitude had erased it. He was going to get what he deserved and more. Right now.

She bent, and filled her hands with cold, spilled spaghetti sauce and flung it at him as she straightened. "Oh, yeah? Well, let's see how *you* like it."

Paul saw determination light her expression, but his subconscious refused to believe what was happening until it was too late. Gooey globs of sauce caught him in the side of the head and trickled down his neck. He yelled like he'd been scalded. "You little brat!"

Belinda was elated. It was high time somebody in Serenity stood up to Paul Randall. How funny he'd looked before he'd realized what she was doing! Laughing till her sides hurt, she saw his expression sobering. He cast around, finally reaching for the sugar bowl on the kitchen table, then lifting it above her head.

Belinda ducked and backed away, her arms raised to ward him off. "I'm warning you. Don't you dare, or..."

"Or what?" Paul's large hand closed around her wrist, held her fast in spite of her struggle to escape. "What will you do? Tell dear old Sam? Ooh, I'm scared."

Sam was the *last* person Belinda wanted to tell about her willing participation in such a childish tussle. "I don't need anybody to help me get the best of you, mister," she shouted. "I can do it alone."

"Oh, yeah?"

"Yeah." With her free hand she reached up to spread the sauce across his cheek, adding to the mess because her fingers were still coated with red, too.

Paul immediately upended the sugar bowl over her head, then let her go with a sarcastic remark, "There, darlin'. That should help you be a little sweeter."

"Why, you..." Belinda felt as if he'd dumped a whole pail of grit in her hair. Sugar granules were trickling over her scalp and down her neck like sand in an hourglass. Without thinking, she squeezed her eyes shut and leaned forward to bat at her loose hair. Unfortunately, she'd forgotten that her fingers were still smeared with sauce. When she realized what she was doing, she began to shake her hands like a kitten who'd just stepped in a dish of milk and didn't know what to do with its wet paws.

"Hey," Paul taunted, "it looks like you're making marinara sauce in your hair. I love that stuff. I usually mix mine in a bowl, though."

Belinda was so furious she was speechless. At that moment it didn't matter to her if they were in someone else's house or not. They'd already made such an awful mess it couldn't get much worse. Paul Randall, however, could get considerably dirtier. She'd see to it. It would serve him right.

Still bent over, her hair hanging down to hide her face, she peered at the assortment of food she'd stacked on the chair. Most of it looked too old and too dry to stick to anything...except maybe whatever treasure lurked in a margarine tub that was within easy reach.

She grabbed the plastic container and popped off the lid, thrilled to see it still held half its original contents. She scooped up a handful of the greasy yellow margarine, straightened with a screech and lunged straight at Paul.

He didn't catch her hands in time to stop the attack. A gob of margarine plopped onto his shoulder. Without hesitation, Belinda smeared what was left of it on his cheek. "There. You've always been too slippery for your own good, anyway. Now you can *slide* your way out of town instead of riding off on that stupid motorcycle of yours."

Jaw clenched, Paul grabbed a red and white whipped cream can from the counter, aimed it at her face and pushed the trigger. The can spit and fizzled ineffectively.

Belinda stood her ground, laughing at his futile efforts to even the score. "You lose."

"Oh, yeah?" He began to shake the can frantically, then turned it upside down. Glaring at her through narrowed eyes, he started to advance, whipped cream nozzle at the ready. "I *never* lose, lady. Not anymore."

Putting up her hands to ward him off, she started to back away. Maybe it was time to call off the hostilities. Judging by the angry, determined look on Paul's face, maybe it was *past* time. Belinda decided to quit while she was ahead. "Truce, truce!"

"Truce, my eye," Paul said menacingly. He wiped his slippery cheek on the sleeve of his shirt and took a slow step toward her. Then another.

She squealed. Ducked. Turned to run. Scrambling, she slipped on the wet floor and lost her balance.

"Crazy woman…" Paul dropped the whipped cream can and lunged to catch her. If his hip hadn't wound up accidentally braced against the counter, their mutual momentum might have carried them both to the floor. Just in time, his arms closed safely around Belinda's waist.

"Let me go," she screeched, twisting and fighting back.

"Hold still and calm down," he countered. "I'm trying to help you."

"Oh, sure, you are." She pounded her fists hard against his chest. "Just like you helped my father's church, right?"

"You never give up, do you?"

Suddenly, the back door slammed. They both froze. Paul wheeled to face the noise, swinging his wriggling burden around with him.

Already short of breath, Belinda gasped. The Whitaker sisters were standing just inside the door, their mouths open, looking totally stunned.

Prudence recovered first. She gave a little squeak, snatched up the nearest cat and clasped it to her breast, holding the poor Siamese so tightly it began yowling and struggling to escape.

Arching one thin, plucked eyebrow and starting to smile, Patience said, "Well, well. Look at the naughty children."

Paul tried to explain. "Aunt Patience, I..."

She ignored him and began to reminisce. "I remember a few food fights Pru and I had when we were girls. But I can see we were rank amateurs compared to you two. We didn't have *nearly* this much fun!"

Chapter Four

Struggling to free herself from Paul's grasp and regain some semblance of dignity, Belinda whispered, "Let me go."

"If you insist." He didn't right her, at first. He also didn't fully release her. Off balance, she started to fall, shrieked and instinctively threw her arms around his neck. Paul steadied her once again. "I thought you wanted me to let you go?"

"I do. I..." Flustered, Belinda made the mistake of looking directly into his eyes. The awareness she saw there took her breath away, made her realize she wasn't the only one feeling momentarily unstable. Unless her imagination was running away with her, Paul was as surprised as she was to be so deeply affected by their physical closeness.

In the background, Patience giggled behind her

hand. "I hope you plan on cleaning up this place before the party tomorrow night. My poor sister washed and waxed the floor just this morning."

"I certainly did," Prudence said, almost in tears. "Whatever possessed you to ruin my beautiful kitchen?"

Paul recovered his emotional and physical balance. Sobering, he carefully set Belinda aside. "It was an accident. We'll take care of it."

"We?" Scowling, Belinda studied him. "I thought you said I was on my own."

"That was before you covered me with sauce," he countered. "Since I'm now as big a mess as you are, I might as well help you."

Belinda decided he had a valid point. Partial imprints of her hands decorated the shoulders and back of his shirt. His collar and chest were dotted with the same dull red, his cheek and right arm were greasy, and he'd had to step into the puddle on the floor to save her from falling. They were in the sauce together.

Paul pulled a handful of paper towels off the roll and spoke to his aunts. "This could take a while. Why don't you both go watch television or something?"

Prudence was more than willing. Muttering to her cat she hurriedly carried it from the kitchen. Patience, however, simply shook her head, pulled a chair as far away from them as she could get without leaving the room and sat down to watch. "Not on your life, Paul, dear," she drawled. "You two go right ahead. I wouldn't miss the rest of your little spat for the world."

He was scowling when he turned to Belinda and said gruffly, "This is all your fault."

"I beg your pardon. I wasn't the one who started it."

"You were, too."

"Was not," she insisted. "*You* made me drop the tomato sauce. Remember?"

"I didn't rub my own face in it," Paul muttered. "And speaking of rubbing my face in something, what did you mean by that crack you made about your father's church?"

"You know very well what I meant."

"Maybe I'm dense. Spell it out for me."

Belinda glanced at Patience and turned aside. "Not now," she told him, keeping her voice low. "This is not the time to discuss it."

"You're absolutely right," he said soberly. "The time we should have discussed it was ten years ago." He abruptly thrust the paper towels at her. "Here. I suggest you start by cleaning yourself off so you don't make things worse."

She jerked the roll out of his hand. "I don't know how it could get much worse. My clothes and shoes are ruined."

"And my shirt isn't?"

"Yeah, well, sorry about that. Guess I lost my temper."

"Tsk tsk. What would your stuffy friends say?"

"That I'm human, just like everybody else."

"And what about good old Sam? What would he say?"

Belinda's breath caught. She'd forgotten all about her promise to meet Sam. "Oh, dear! What time is it?"

Paul glanced at the clock on the far wall. "After seven. Why?"

"I'm missing the council meeting. I promised Sam I'd be there tonight. He'll be really upset when I don't show up."

"So, call the town hall and explain."

Making a wry face, Belinda said, "Oh, sure. That's a great idea. And what do you suggest I tell him?"

One corner of Paul's mouth began to lift as his glance traveled over her. "You have a point there. I suppose it wouldn't do to say you had a slight accident, because then he'd assume you were hurt and want to doctor you. And you certainly can't tell him the whole truth. Or can you?"

"Of course I can," she countered, trying to sound more convinced than she actually was. "Sam's a reasonable person. He'll understand that I had to come here first to deliver Gram's cake. Everything else was accidental."

"Everything?" One dark eyebrow rose.

"Well, almost everything." She eyed the door to

the hall. "I don't dare walk on the carpet to get to the phone in the hall, though."

Paul was quick to offer a solution. "You won't have to go anywhere if you use my cell phone." He looked to his aunt. "I left it out in the car. Would you mind?"

Patience smiled sweetly and got to her feet. "Not at all, dear. As long as you promise you two won't do anything else exciting while I'm gone."

Blushing, Belinda bent to pick up the whipped cream can and said the first thing that came to mind. "Don't worry. I'm sure Paul will behave himself from now on."

The moment the words were out of her mouth she realized she might have inadvertently rekindled his antagonistic attitude. Uneasy, she glanced at him. Instead of taking offense, however, he'd resumed his unemotional, professional demeanor. That was too bad. Even as a youth he'd always taken life too seriously. The times she'd managed to get him to relax enough to smile and be candid were some of her fondest memories. Even the food fight they'd just had was better than seeing him sulk.

Moving mechanically, Belinda wiped off her hands, slipped out of her shoes and padded to the sink to wash. She was drying her hands and forearms when Patience returned with the portable phone and gingerly handed it to her.

"Thank you." Hoping that Sam would have his telephone in his pocket, as usual, Belinda dialed the number from memory. He answered almost immediately.

"Belinda? Where are you? The meeting's started."

"At the Whitakers'. I was de—"

"What are you doing there?" he interrupted.

"As I was trying to tell you, I stopped here to deliver a cake for Gram and I got delayed."

Sam's voice became a whisper. "All right. No harm done. Are you on your way now?"

"No. I—I don't think I'll be able to make it."

"What are you talking about? Just tell the old ladies you have to go and walk out the door."

"It's not as simple as that," she said softly, cupping the small phone in her hands and mimicking Sam's hushed tone.

Before she could explain, Paul called loudly to her. "Hey, Belinda, do you want me to throw your shoes away or are you going to try to salvage them?"

She covered the mouthpiece with her hand. "Hush."

"Why?" Paul asked, raising his voice even more. "You said you were going to tell him everything."

"Not now!" she countered. "He's in a meeting."

"What difference does that make?" Paul was beside her in three rapid strides. He held out his hand. "Here. Give me the phone. I'll take care of it."

Belinda resisted. "I'll bet you will."

"Look. Do you trust him or not?" Paul challenged.

"Of course I do."

"Then there shouldn't be a problem."

The only way to prove her faith in Sam was to hand over the phone. By the time Sam asked, "What's going on there?" he was talking to Paul.

"Nothing important," Paul answered calmly. "Your girlfriend just had a little accident with some spaghetti sauce." He paused. "That's right." He listened for a moment. "No, we weren't eating it. We were flinging it at each other. Believe me, you don't want her showing up at that meeting looking like she does now." He chuckled wryly. "Too much garlic. The sugar I added didn't seem to sweeten her up much, either."

Belinda couldn't hear Sam's reply, but judging by the smug look on Paul's face she imagined it was pretty colorful.

"No, no," Paul said. "You stay right there. She'll be fine. We'll take good care of her. If she decides she can't drive home the way she is, I'll get one of my aunts to loan her something else to wear. That should be an interesting sight, don't you think?"

Wide-eyed, Belinda watched Paul begin to grin as he listened. Then he said, "Same to you," and pressed the button to break the connection.

Hands on her hips, she waited impatiently. "Well? What did Sam say?"

Paul shook his head. "Word for word? Believe

me, you don't want me to repeat it." He looked at the clock. "I figure we have about ten minutes, tops, before he charges in here to rescue you, so let's get to work on this mess. Half the blame is yours. I don't intend to get stuck cleaning up all by myself."

"You really think Sam will come to my rescue?" The notion made her feel surprisingly special.

"I don't know about him," Paul said flatly. "But if you were my girl and I'd gotten a call that you were in trouble, *I* would."

When Paul finally went outside to get a second trash can, Belinda took advantage of his absence to slip off her panty hose and throw them away. Disappointed, she sighed deeply. Paul had been wrong about Sam showing up. Almost two hours had passed with no sign of the doctor, and they were done with the basic cleaning. Thankfully, they'd been able to keep the peace while they worked.

Patience had been upset when Paul had insisted that they dispose of so many leftovers. Eventually, she'd stopped arguing and gone to join her sister in the den.

Terribly weary all of a sudden, Belinda leaned against the edge of the counter, closed her eyes and talked to God while she waited for Paul to return. "Oh, Father. It's been ten years since I prayed for that impossible man to come back to me. I've changed my mind. You know I have. Please, please tell me You're not answering that old prayer *now*."

The screen banged noisily. Her eyes popped open. Paul had shed his stained dress shirt, leaving only his plain white T-shirt and denim jeans. His hair was mussed, his dark eyes bright. It ought to be against the law to look that appealing, Belinda mused, annoyed that she'd noticed in the first place. When he began to smile a little she was glad she had the kitchen counter to lean on.

"You look beat," he said with a resigned sigh. "Why don't you go on home. I'll finish up here."

"I can't. I still have to mop the floor."

"I'll do that, too."

"Oh, sure."

Paul chuckled softly. "Trust me. Thanks to a hitch in the Navy, I'm a real expert with a mop."

That was a surprise. "You were in the service?"

"Uh-huh. I joined because it seemed like the best way to further my education." *And to get far away from my past,* he thought.

"I'm impressed."

"Well, don't be. I hated every minute of it. I never was real good at taking orders."

Belinda's weariness helped lower her guard so that she spoke more from her heart than from her head. "No kidding. You used to be a terrible rebel. I think that was one of the things I liked best about you."

"What?" His brow knit. "Why?"

"I don't know. Maybe because I'd led such a sheltered life. My father had a lot of strict rules about how his only daughter should behave. I was always afraid of accidentally breaking one of those rules. When I met you, I saw what it was like to have freedom, to enjoy life.''

Paul's loud, abrupt response made her jump. ''Ha! I'd have given anything to have a father who cared where I was and what I was doing. Just a normal, everyday dad. A guy who fit in and acted like everybody else's father.''

Stunned, Belinda paused to sort out her thoughts. ''I'm sorry. I guess I never understood. I knew your dad had problems. We all knew. I just assumed you *wanted* to be different.''

''Why? Because I acted like I didn't care?'' Snorting with self-derision, he crossed the kitchen to bring her the empty trash can. As he set it down, a plaintive mewing diverted his attention. One of the black-and-white kittens seemed to be wedged in the narrow space between the refrigerator and the end of the cabinet.

When he reached down to rescue it, it hissed at him. ''Hey, this little guy's got guts.'' Paul held the shivering kitten to his warm chest and petted it to soothe it. ''He's so scared he's about to shake apart, but he knew he couldn't run away so he stood up to me.''

In awe, Belinda softly asked, ''Is that how *you* felt? About having to live in Serenity, I mean.''

Paul saw pity in her eyes. Pity and welling tears. He wanted neither. Especially not from her. Disgusted with himself for accidentally letting down his defenses, he sought to remedy the situation. "Of course not. I was talking about this cat. What did you think I meant?"

"Nothing. I didn't realize you'd changed the subject, that's all." She reached out. "Better give him to me. He's leaving little footprints all over your shirt. He must have stepped in a spot of sauce that we missed."

Paul reluctantly did as she asked. "Okay. As long as you don't intend to try to give him a bath."

"Of course not. I'll just wipe his paws with a damp cloth so he doesn't track up the floor. He and his mama can do the rest." Moving slowly and murmuring endearments to the frightened kitty she made her way to the sink, squeezed out one of the kitchen towels they'd used to wipe down the cabinets and gently washed its feet.

"There you go. See?" she crooned. "That didn't hurt a bit, did it?" Cradling the kitten against her with one hand she turned her attention to Paul and began to dab at the faint, tiny paw prints on his T-shirt with a corner of the damp towel.

"Leave it alone. It's okay," he insisted.

"It'll just take a second...."

Paul's hand closed around hers, stilling her efforts.

Confused, Belinda raised her eyes to meet his. He didn't speak. He didn't have to. The look in his eyes was warning enough. It sent prickles shivering over her skin and raised the fine hairs on her arms into goose bumps.

Time sputtered to a standstill, pausing until the kitten mewed a plaintive distraction. As soon as Belinda broke eye contact with Paul to glance down, the intimate mood was broken.

"I'll take him," Paul said, releasing his hold and pushing her hand away while relieving her of the tiny ball of fur. "You'd better get going. It's late."

Yes, she thought sadly. *It's way too late...for a lot of things.*

Especially for her and Paul Randall.

That was the heartbreaking part.

Belinda didn't remember any details of her trip home. She didn't even realize she'd arrived until she automatically turned left into her own driveway.

Her car's headlights swept across a parked red Camaro. Evidently, Sam had decided to avoid confronting Paul and had gone to her place to wait instead. *Terrific.* She knew she should feel delighted to see him, but in truth, he was the last person she wanted to talk to right now. She also knew she had no choice.

Heaving a sigh of resignation, Belinda climbed out of her car and started for the front porch. In the yellow glare of the porch light she could see Sam on the top step. The night was warm, clear and humid. He'd shed his suit coat and tie and rolled up the sleeves of his shirt.

"Hi," Belinda said. "The back door's unlocked. You could have gone inside where you'd be more comfortable. I have to leave the air conditioner on or the house gets so hot I'd never get it cooled down enough to sleep comfortably."

"No way. Out here is fine."

She assumed he was being solicitous of her spotless reputation. "How sweet."

"What is?" Sam frowned at her as she climbed the steps toward him, then stood aside so she could unlock the door.

"Worrying about what other people will think of me if they see you acting too at home here. Once a rumor like that gets started it's almost impossible to stop, especially in a close-knit town like Serenity."

"I suppose you're right. I hadn't thought of that. I stopped by to make sure you were all right and decided to stay out here because I heard Snuffy barking. You left her loose in the house. You know how I feel about that dog."

"Oh." What a disappointment. Belinda paused at the door, blocking his entry and making sure her overly friendly beagle didn't charge out and jump all over him. "I'm sorry, Sam. It's late, and I'm beat. I'm not going to ask you in."

Sam sounded disgusted. "Why not? You just spent hours at the Whitakers' with Randall. *That* certainly won't help your reputation."

"We weren't alone. Besides, it couldn't be helped." Watching the doctor's glance take in her soiled, disheveled appearance, she ordered, "Stop staring at me like that. You look like you just bit into a wild persimmon before the first hard winter freeze."

"What's that supposed to mean?"

"Sorry. I forgot you aren't from around here. Wild persimmons are real sour, like the look on your face. The frost makes them sweet."

Shoving his hands into his pockets, Sam apologized. "Okay. I'm sorry, too. I suppose this is partly my fault. I did tell you to talk to Randall whenever you got the chance." He raised an eyebrow and stopped scowling. "So, what did you find out?"

That he knows how to mop a floor and likes kittens, Belinda thought. She said, "We didn't talk about the sale of the house at all, I'm afraid. We spent the entire time cleaning up the food I spilled trying to get Gram's cake to fit into Miss Prudence's refrigerator." She gestured at her skirt. "As you can see, it was a terrible mess."

"That's an understatement."

The disappointment in Sam's expression told her far more about his true disposition than she wanted to know. When he gently laid his hands on her shoulders and bent to kiss her, she presented her cheek. "Good night, Sam."

"Good night, honey." He hesitated as if he might say more, then wheeled and started for his car. "Remember, I'll pick you up at six-thirty tomorrow evening."

The balmy night air wasn't warm enough to keep Belinda from shivering as she watched him drive away. She folded her arms across her chest and hugged herself. In all the confusion she'd forgotten their dinner date.

Normally, she enjoyed Sam's company. Ever since Paul had returned, however, she was beginning to feel like a tasty bone being fought over by two hungry, possessive dogs, each tugging her in opposite directions. There were already imaginary teeth marks on her poor, confused psyche.

And speaking of dogs… Now that Sam had gone, it was safe to let Snuffy out. "Come on, baby. The coast is clear," she said, opening the door all the way and bending to greet her loving pet. Panting and leaping at Belinda, the brown, white and black beagle dashed onto the porch.

"I'm glad to see you, too." Belinda chuckled. Nose to the ground, Snuffy was instinctively following tracks. She circled the place where Sam had stood, then trailed him to the driveway, stopping where he'd gotten into his car. Apparently satisfied, she gave a sharp, resonant bark and bounded back to Belinda.

"Yes, girl, he's gone." Belinda ruffled the dog's pendulous ears while it eagerly sniffed the hem of her skirt. "That's spaghetti sauce. And you can probably tell I was around a few cats, too."

Snuffy wagged her tail and cocked her head, looking at her mistress expectantly. "No, baby. I didn't bring you a kitty to play with, although that may not be such a bad idea. At least you'd have somebody to keep you company while I'm at work." Belinda's voice softened, sounded more like she was speaking to a child. "Are you lonesome when I'm gone, sweetheart? Huh? Are you?"

The exuberant dog began licking her bare toes. "Hey! Stop that. It tickles," she said with a soft laugh. "If you're trying to tell me I need a bath, you're right. Come on. I'm putting you in the back yard where you can't get into trouble. Then I'm going to treat myself to a long, long shower. I've certainly earned it."

With a series of short, happy barks, the little beagle dashed around the house ahead of Belinda and darted through the open gate, skidding to a stop next to its red plastic food dish.

Amused, Belinda grinned and nodded as she latched the gate behind her and headed for the back door. "Okay. You win. First, I'll feed the dog."

And then I'll crash, she added, noting once again how tired she was. Must be from all the hard scrubbing and cleaning she'd had to do.

Her conscience immediately contradicted her. Who was she kidding? She was beat because she'd spent so much time dealing with Paul…with her reactions to him.

Belinda started to mentally argue, then stopped. There was no use denying that a spark of affection remained between them. But that was all it was. All it could ever be. When their lives had briefly converged ten years ago, they might have had a chance to find a happy middle ground. But no more. Paul had his successful law practice and the perfect new life he'd worked so hard to make for himself in Harrison. And she had Serenity, the only place where she'd ever felt truly at home.

The last thing Paul wanted to do was go back.

The last thing she wanted to do was go forward.

Chapter Five

Sam didn't say anything about her choice of clothing when he picked her up for their dinner engagement, but Belinda was certain he noticed she wasn't wearing the simple black sheath he'd suggested.

To be fair, she had gotten it out of the closet and considered it, but she just didn't feel like being so somber. This was summer in the Ozarks. Bright color was everywhere. Most people had a myriad of beautiful flowers in their yards, or filling planter boxes, or cascading over the sides of baskets hung in the shade of old-fashioned covered porches like hers. Some gardeners, Eloise included, had all three. And a lush vegetable garden, to boot.

Besides, the black sheath was a terrible choice for hot, muggy weather, and today's temperature had been particularly high. Belinda figured it was bad enough that she had to wear panty hose. She wasn't about to purposely make herself even more uncomfortable.

That line of reasoning had led her to pick out a pale pink sleeveless dress with a short, open-knit jacket in a darker rose. The outfit was far from businesslike. It was, however, pretty. And cool. It also set off the reddish glint in her hair, and she felt good wearing it. That was the most important thing.

When they arrived at the Whitaker mansion, she was doubly glad she'd dressed lightly. Sam parked beneath an enormous walnut tree that grew next to the driveway, but the temperature was still uncomfortably high, even in the shade.

"Whew!" Belinda fanned herself with her hand as she climbed out of the car. "I'm afraid working in an air-conditioned office has spoiled me."

"Yeah. Me, too." Sam used his folded handkerchief to blot beads of perspiration from his forehead. He took her elbow, urging her toward the elaborate, once regal porch. "Come on. Let's get inside before we melt."

"I don't think I've ever gone in the front door here," she said candidly. "When I was little, Gram used to bring me by to visit Miss Prudence all the time. I'd usually sit on the back porch and eat her homemade sugar cookies while she and Gram talked."

Sam was already banging the brass knocker. "That's nice. But you need to remember this is not a social call. Keep your mind on the reason we're here."

"To get the Whitaker sisters to sell the place to you and your partners. I know." She made a face at him. "Don't you think it's about time you told me what your plans are?"

"When I'm ready." Sam raised his arm to rap again just as the door swung open.

Belinda watched his countenance rapidly darken. Her gaze instinctively followed his. The humid air became cloying. Nearly unbreathable. When Paul smiled at her, she felt suddenly faint.

"Come in, come in," Paul said, stepping out of the way. "Glad you could make it."

Sam shook his hand. Belinda refrained. By using Sam as a buffer, she was able to enter the house gracefully while still managing to avoid Paul's touch. Thankfully, he didn't seem to notice the slight.

Acting the affable host, Paul led the way into the formal parlor. High ceilings helped cool the room by giving the rising warmer air a place to go. Portable electric fans were strategically placed to stir the cooler air below.

The Whitaker sisters were seated together on the brocade settee. An older man Belinda didn't recognize was the sixth person in the room. Paul introduced him as Milton Boggs, a friend from Harrison, but Belinda suspected there was an ulterior motive for his presence. Evidently, Sam felt that way, too, because he eyed the thin, balding man with suspicion.

"So, what brings you to Serenity?" Sam asked him as they politely shook hands.

Boggs shrugged casually. "Not much. It is nice to get away once in awhile. See the sights. Serenity is a lovely town. You must be thankful you chose to bring your medical practice here."

"I am. I intend to spend the rest of my life here." He drew Belinda closer to his side. "You know. Settle down. Get married. Raise a family."

She stiffened. Glanced at Paul. Nothing in his expression indicated that Sam's declaration had upset him. Either he truly didn't care or he was very good at masking his feelings. Maybe both.

Sam escorted her to a chair across the room and stood beside it like a sentry on guard duty. Looking for some way to relieve the tension, Belinda noticed the items on the tea cart and smiled at Prudence. "I was just telling Sam about your wonderful sugar cookies. I see you've made some."

"Yes. Mayor Smith phoned and said he was going to be late so I decided to serve these while we wait. Sister made the lemonade. Would you like a glass?"

"Yes, please."

Patience put ice cubes into a tumbler and filled it with lemonade. Before Sam had a chance to offer to fetch it for her, Paul had taken on the task. He also put two cookies on a napkin, then delivered everything with a polite smile. "Here you go. How about you, Doc? Lemonade?"

"No, thanks."

Belinda had to concentrate hard to keep her hand from trembling as she took the glass and cookies from Paul. It helped that he was looking at Sam instead of at her. She perched on the edge of the chair, napkin in her lap, and smiled woodenly.

"You look a bit peaked," Patience observed. "Are you feeling all right?"

"I'm fine." Belinda wasn't about to admit she hadn't felt light-headed until she'd encountered Paul again. She took a sip of lemonade and peered at him over the rim of the frosty glass. He looked so cool, so unruffled. His slacks were pressed, his shirt was crisp and white and his smile was enigmatic.

She pulled a face, disgusted with herself for paying so much attention to him. Being attracted to Paul Randall in the first place, in spite of herself, then being thrust into such close proximity to him, was liable to make this one of the most difficult evenings she'd ever spent.

"Oh, dear," Prudence said, noting the change in Belinda's expression. "Sister didn't forget to add sugar again, did she?"

Paul answered for her. "No, Aunt Pru. I tasted the lemonade. It's perfect, as usual." A knowing grin spread across his face. "I think Ms. Carnes may be reliving the little problem she had in your kitchen yesterday."

"*I* had? And what do you mean, *little* problem?" Belinda bristled. "That was a full-blown disaster, and you know it."

"I have to agree with you there," he gibed. "I wish I'd thought to grab my camera and snap a picture of you."

The image that immediately flashed into Belinda's mind was one of Paul, staring at her photo and dreaming, just as she'd often done with an old high school picture of him.

Paul saw a softening of her expression, a glassy shimmer in her lovely blue eyes, and he wondered what she was thinking. Whatever it was, he didn't think it was wise to ask. Especially not in front of Sam. Instead, he said, "Sure. I might need that kind of solid evidence for blackmail some day."

Belinda made another disgusted face. "What would you charge me with? Breaking and entering?"

"Nope. Just breaking...jar breaking." He started to chuckle. "And maybe butter smearing, if I could find a legal precedent for it."

Belinda was relieved when the mayor finally arrived and everyone gathered in the formal dining room. Its flowered wallpaper was faded, and the drapes were a bit frayed at the hem, but it was still easy to envision how elegant the room had once looked. Unless she missed her guess, the mahogany table and chairs were Chippendale.

The caterers had set up their silver serving dishes on a massive matching sideboard and were standing beside it, waiting to begin.

"This is beautiful," Belinda told the elderly sisters as she admired the lavishly set table. "I didn't know you had such fancy china and crystal."

"The silverware was Mother's," Patience said proudly. "And she helped me collect the china for my hope chest. The stemware was our aunt Nettie's."

"Yes," Prudence agreed. "She willed it to both of us and we hated to split up the set, so I gave my half to Sister."

"Not that it made one whit of difference," Patience observed, beginning to pout. "Since neither one of us ever left home, it's stayed right here, anyway."

"Oh, and I suppose that's *my* fault? Nobody told you you couldn't leave."

Belinda had never known the sisters to act so openly antagonistic. Of course she usually saw them separately, especially since Grandma Eloise was closer friends with Prudence. Unsure of what to say next, she looked to Paul. It was obvious that he, too, was surprised by their mutual outburst.

"Well," Paul offered, his voice calm and even, "neither of you will have the problem for much longer, once you sell the house."

"That's another thing," Prudence said stiffly. "I don't care what my sister decides to do or where she wants to go. I've given the matter a lot of thought and I'm perfectly content right here. I'm not leaving."

"It's those stupid cats of hers," Patience explained. "She's afraid they won't be happy anywhere else." She huffed and plunked down into the chair Paul had pulled out for her. "Sister never did have the sense God gave a goat when it came to dumb animals."

"Oh? Well, at least my animals can be trusted to never turn on me. Not like some people I might mention."

"You wouldn't know a friend if she came up and bit you," Patience argued.

"*My* friends don't bite."

"You know very well what I meant," her sister countered. "If you'd get out once in a while you might actually enjoy yourself the way I do."

"I wouldn't want to be like you if that was the only choice in the world," Prudence said, her voice shrill. "All you ever think about is yourself."

"That's not true, and you know it!"

Paul tried to call a peaceful halt to the argument by holding up his hands. When that didn't work, he put two fingers in his mouth and whistled. Everyone froze.

"That's better," he said with a tolerant smile. He signaled the caterers to begin serving. "I think we'd better eat. The soup is probably getting cold."

"We didn't order soup." Patience sounded miffed.

Paul laughed softly and shook his head, looking from one of his testy aunts to the other. "I know we didn't. But if I thought it would quiet you two down, I'd go open a can of the stuff and fix it myself. Now, can we eat in peace? Please?"

"If that's what you want, dear," Patience said amiably. Her sister merely nodded in sullen agreement.

How different the two women were, Belinda mused. She'd always thought it would be loads of fun to have a twin. Watching the Whitaker sisters interact was starting to make her thankful she was an only child.

But it would be nice to have somebody else she could feel close to besides Gram, she thought. A contemporary who truly cared and understood her. Someone who belonged to her and she to them. A sense of belonging was one of the things that had blessed her so when she'd given her life to Jesus. No matter where she was or how bad the circumstances seemed to be, He was always there. Always ready to help.

All she had to do was get her pride out of the way, stop being stubborn, and surrender to His will. It sounded like a simple enough act. It wasn't.

Sometimes, like now, when she was so confused by her rampant feelings that she hardly knew her own name, it was practically inconceivable.

* * *

During dinner, Belinda was relieved that Mayor Smith chose to distract everyone by telling tales of Serenity in its early days. She'd heard various versions of his stories often, which was just as well, since she couldn't have paid close attention if her life had depended upon it. Eating her dinner with Paul seated directly across the table was hard enough. Taking part in a discussion that required the assimilation and processing of unfamiliar information would have been impossible.

"'Course, I was just a boy back then," the mayor said, "but I do recall the way this place here looked. It was the finest estate in the whole county, maybe even the whole state of Arkansas. Had everything, a big house, fine stables, grand gardens..." He paused to blot perspiration from his balding pate with a folded handkerchief. "It had the best kitchen garden, too. Me and a couple of other boys used to dare each other to swipe watermelons out of it. We used to sneak in from the back side, off of Old Sturkey Road. Nowadays, I'd be lucky to be able to *walk* that far—" he patted his paunch "—let alone run, totin' a humongous melon!"

Patience covered her mouth delicately with her napkin and tittered. "You should have seen those boys! I used to hide with Papa and watch from up in the carriage house loft. He got the biggest kick out of it. Especially watching you, Ira."

The mayor gasped. "He knew?"

"Of course, he did. It was a game to him. That was why Sister and I were always needling you to do it again."

Belinda had held her tongue as long as she could. "That doesn't seem like a very good way to raise children. It sounds to me like he was condoning stealing."

"I suppose it does, these days," Patience answered, thoughtful. "But back then Papa gave away lots more than our family ate. Everybody knew all they had to do was ask and they could have whatever they needed."

Looking relieved, the mayor wiped his brow again. "That's true. Come to think of it, I suppose that's why my pa never whipped me for doing it. Anyway, I turned out all right, so I guess no harm was done."

Belinda noticed a mischievous twinkle lighting Patience's grayish-blue eyes. "Well, I don't know about that, Ira," the older woman drawled, "you *did* become a politician."

Laughter filled the room. Forgetting herself, Belinda made the mistake of relaxing her guard and looking at Paul.

His eyebrows arched in acknowledgment and challenge. "Just goes to prove you never can tell, doesn't it?"

Before Belinda could decide how best to respond, Prudence jumped to her feet and grasped the edge of the table. "Stop talking about hiding and spying on people! All of you. It's not funny, it's a mean, nasty habit, especially when a person's own family is involved.'' The color drained from her face.

"Aunt Prudence..." Paul was beside her in seconds. "Are you all right?"

"No. I'm not all right," she wailed. "I just wish... Oh, dear..." When Paul put his arm around her shoulders she hid her face against his chest.

He stroked her thin back. "This whole business about selling the house has been hard on everybody. You're probably overtired. If you've finished eating, why don't we let Aunt Patience take you up to your room so you can get some rest?"

"No! Not her," Prudence cried. "She's the worst of them all."

Paul was at a loss. He looked at Sam. "In that case, would you mind checking her out, Doctor? I've never seen my aunt act like this, before."

"Humpf," Patience said, making a sour face. "I have. Plenty of times. Don't worry. There's not a thing wrong with her that gettin' her own way won't cure. She just wants to distract us, keep us from talking about the sale of this monstrosity of a house."

Sam got to his feet. "Well, as far as I'm concerned, she's been successful. I can't see any reason to continue negotiations when one of the primary parties to the deal is so unwilling to sell that she's making herself sick over it." He rounded the end of the table and reached for Prudence's wrist, timed her heartbeats, then looked at Paul. "She's a little over-wrought, but her pulse is strong and steady. I can prescribe a mild sedative if you want."

"I don't need any pills," Prudence insisted, snif-fling. "I'll just go lie down for a bit and I'll be fine."

Paul hesitated to release her. Instead, he started to guide her from the room. She shook off his touch. "I can manage." Lifting her misty gaze, she blinked back tears. "I want you to stay right here and be my lawyer, like you promised. Make sure Sister doesn't pull another one of her dirty tricks and sell my house out from under me."

"You know she wouldn't do that, Aunt Pru."

"Ha!" Prudence glowered at her twin through reddened eyes. "Don't kid yourself, boy. There are lots of things she'd do, given half a chance. I should know. I've spent the last eighty-some years watch-ing her do them."

Sam took Paul's place beside Prudence. "I'll han-dle this," he said. "You come, too, Belinda. Miss Whitaker and I are going to go have a little chat, and I want you there. I think you'll find it interest-ing."

"Of course." Belinda didn't care for Sam's over-bearing attitude. However, she did want to help calm Prudence down, so she gently cupped the woman's elbow and followed his orders. He was *not* at his most likable when he was acting so superior or hint-ing that there was some cloak-and-dagger plot afoot.

She'd much rather he'd have simply said whatever he intended to say and gotten it over with, instead of drawing her away from the others.

Others? Belinda countered silently. *You mean Paul Randall, don't you?* Of course she did. He was the reason she didn't want to leave the party, didn't want to go up to Prudence's room with Sam.

Sighing, she sobered. Sam might not realize it, but he'd been wise to take her away from the man she had once loved. The more time she spent with Paul the more she rued the mistakes of the past. The more she wished she could somehow make amends.

Was *that* why the Lord had brought him back to Serenity? she wondered abruptly. Was she supposed to show him how to forgive all the people, including herself, who had accused him and driven him out of town?

Disgusted, Belinda huffed. Fat chance. You can't very well teach it if you can't *do* it, and she was still furious with Paul. As much as she hated to admit it, she was also holding a grudge against her late father for having stood between them. Which meant she was far from the ideal example of Christian love.

Some peacemaker! God wasn't going to use her to lead *anybody* down the path to forgiveness and harmony until she'd mastered the concept herself.

Maybe by the time she was as old as the Whitaker sisters she'd have figured it all out. Then again, maybe it was going to take her even longer.

Lost in thought, Belinda escorted Prudence up the

winding staircase to her second-floor bedroom. Sam followed.

"I'm glad you agreed to come up here with us, Miss Whitaker," Sam said, closing the door behind all three of them. "I've been wanting to speak with you in private."

Prudence snorted in obvious disgust. "Ha! Don't start tryin' to sweet-talk me, Sam Barryman. I'm wise to men's tricks. I may look older than dirt but I'm far from senile. This house is not for sale. Period."

Back ramrod straight, chin jutting out, she plopped down on the edge of the bed and crossed her arms defensively, looking for all the world like a naughty child who'd been sent to her room for misbehaving.

Sam ambled over to join her. Leaning against the carved post that held up the bed's canopy, he said, "I don't want your house, Miss Whitaker."

That was a surprise to Belinda. Curiosity got the better of her. "You don't? But I thought…"

"You thought what I wanted everybody to think," Sam said smugly. "Actually, it's only the vacant property I'm interested in. I couldn't care less about this old wreck of a house. It's more of a liability than an asset."

Belinda stared at Sam, then looked at Prudence. Compared to her present ashen complexion, she hadn't been a bit pale before. "You…you don't want my house?"

"No. I don't. I intend to build a clinic and a small hospital on this site. We all know Serenity desperately needs adequate medical facilities. Think of it. We might even name the place after your family."

Prudence grew pensive. "I suppose Father would have liked that." A faraway look filled her eyes. Her voice grew thready. "I always listened to Father. My sister didn't, but I did. When Father said Eldon wasn't good enough for me, I sent him away."

Sam shot a questioning look at Belinda. Confused, she shrugged and said, "This is the first I've heard about anything like that, Miss Prudence. Did it happen a long time ago?"

"Long time?" The elderly woman sighed deeply. "Yes. A very long time ago." Another heart-wrenching sigh. "Eldon loved me. I know he did. If *she* hadn't interfered I'm sure I could have convinced Father to give us his blessing."

Prudence snapped to the present. "Sister can't be trusted. Never could. That's why I don't believe she only wants to sell this place so she can run off and travel. She's got something else up her sleeve. Well, whatever it is, she's not going to get away with it." Her frigid gaze lit on the doctor. "And neither are you, mister."

None of the guests could help overhearing the loudest of the conversation coming from the floor above. The party broke up when the mayor excused himself and Patience talked Milton Boggs into taking a stroll in the garden with her.

Paul politely walked everyone to the door, then returned to the foot of the staircase and quietly bowed his head to listen. All was quiet. Apparently, Prudence had calmed down. What a shame she was so upset with her sister. He wished he could think of some way to reconcile them.

Belinda started down the stairs. She paused at the landing when she spotted Paul at the bottom. If she hadn't been on a mercy mission she would have waited until he'd walked away so she wouldn't have to pass right by him. Unfortunately, any delay was likely to cause Sam to come looking for her, which would only complicate matters.

Steeling herself for the encounter with Paul, she stood tall and announced her presence as she continued to descend. "Miss Prudence is having trouble resting. I'm going out to the car for Sam's medical bag."

The sound of Belinda's voice gave Paul a jolt. His head snapped up. He watched her approach with his heart in his throat. She'd never looked lovelier. Every time he saw her he had the same kind of gut-level reaction, the same kind of thoughts. She was floating down the stairs like a vision from his dreams, coming to him quickly, surely, the way he'd so often fantasized she would.

Her steps slowed as she reached the ground floor. The hand she'd placed on the smooth banister slid to a stop, bumping against his. The contact sent a tingle up her arm that tickled the fine hairs at the back of her neck and made her shiver.

Paul jerked his hand away. "I'll get the bag for you. Just tell me what it looks like."

"I'm not sure." Jiggling the set of car keys in her hand, she smiled. "Sam said it was in the trunk. With luck, there's only one bag to choose from."

When Paul reached to take the keys from her, she held them away. "Uh-uh. Sam's very particular about his car. I'm the only other person allowed to touch it."

"How special," Paul taunted. "Does he let you polish it, too?"

"As a matter of fact, we did give it a fresh coat of wax recently. It was one of those balmy evenings a week or so before this heat wave started."

"That figures." He couldn't help smirking. "Want to polish *my* car? You're obviously a pro."

"In your dreams, Randall," she countered, breezing past him and heading for the front door.

By the time Belinda returned with Sam's medical bag, Paul was nowhere to be seen. To her dismay, she was terribly disappointed he hadn't waited for her.

Nevertheless, she whispered, "Thank you, Father. You know better than I do what's best for me. I just wish..." She broke off. "Never mind, Lord. You rescued me from that man once. I'm not going to put myself in the position where You have to do it again.''

Pausing at the foot of the stairs, her hand on the banister, she waited for the sense of peace she'd grown to expect when she relinquished control of her life to the Lord.

This time, it didn't come.

Chapter Six

By the following morning, Belinda had managed to rationalize away her uneasy feelings about being thrust into the latest situation involving Paul Randall. One of her biggest failings had always been trying to figure out what God had in mind for her long before He was ready to reveal it. This time, she was determined to avoid making that mistake.

She wasn't, however, ready to sit by and watch the Whitaker sisters lose out on a chance for a rosy future simply because one of them was suffering from emotional problems. Before she could implement her plan to telephone her grandmother and ask for background information, the older woman showed up at the Chamber office on her own. Belinda took it as a good sign.

"I'm glad you stopped by," she told Eloise, giving her a hug. "I was going to phone you."

"Phone me about what, dear?"

"The party at the Whitakers' last night."

Eloise brightened. "Oh, goodie. I'm dying to hear all the juicy details. How did it go? Was my cake a success?"

"The cake was wonderful, as usual. I hardly got a chance to taste it before Sam and I had to take Miss Prudence up to her room, though."

"Oh, dear! Was she sick?"

"Not exactly. Unless acting weird counts. One minute she seemed fine and the next she was nearly hysterical. She kept rambling on about how awful Patience was. Sam finally had to give her an injection so she could rest."

"Poor Pru. I knew she was getting worse, but I had no idea she'd regressed that far."

Folding her arms across her chest, Belinda said, "I think it's time you told me exactly what's going on."

"I don't know if I should."

"Well, I do. Sam says the poor woman's liable to have a nervous breakdown if we don't figure out what's really bothering her and help her deal with it. As her best friend, I figure you must know."

"Well… Okay." Eloise followed Belinda to her windowless office and sank into the nearest chair. "I suppose it's too late for the story to do any more damage than it already has."

Belinda pulled up another chair. "Is it something

really bad? The way Prudence was carrying on last night, you'd think Patience had committed murder.''

''I suppose it does seem like a terrible crime to Pru. She was never the same after Eldon Lafferty jilted her.''

''She did mention someone named Eldon.''

Eloise nodded. ''He was the Whitakers' gardener. He and Prudence had a lot in common, a love for plants, an uncanny understanding of animals—they even went to the same little church. The problem was, Mr. Whitaker didn't consider a gardener to be a suitable match for his daughter and he told her so.'' She paused, smiling wistfully. ''Things were different back in those days. Folks set a lot of store by the unwritten rules of society. And young women obeyed their fathers.''

''Surely, when Prudence got older...''

''By that time, it was too late,'' Eloise said. ''Eldon was long gone.''

''But why is she so mad at Patience?''

''Because Patience stole Eldon away from her right before everything came to a head. I think that was what made old man Whitaker so mad. He couldn't stand seeing *both* of his daughters smitten.''

''How awful. For everybody.''

''No kidding. I don't suppose poor Eldon even knew what hit him when Patience started to flirt with him. You know how she is. She's never done anything halfway. And Pru's always been shy, so she didn't know how to fight back. When she lost the man she loved, first to her sister and then to fate, she became sort of a recluse. If it hadn't been for her teaching job, I don't think she'd have set foot out of that house again.''

Touched, Belinda shook her head. ''What finally happened to the gardener?''

''Nobody knows. Word was that the girls' father paid him off and sent him away. Pru never heard a word from him. To save face, she started telling everybody she was the one who'd told him to go.''

The sad story was painfully reminiscent of Belinda's loss of Paul. Thoughtful, she sighed. ''I suppose it's way too late to try to find Mr. Lafferty and bring him back.''

Eloise gasped. ''Don't you dare! That wouldn't accomplish a thing except to start the feud all over again. Pru is sure Eldon would have come to his senses and admitted he still loved her if he'd stayed in Serenity. When Patience got herself involved with him she ruined everything. There's no way to change that.''

''I guess you're right. I just wish I knew how we're going to help Miss Prudence let go of the past and begin to enjoy her life.''

Eloise snorted. ''How do you know she isn't enjoying it? Just because she chooses to be a loner doesn't mean she isn't happy. She loves her cats, she gardens some when her health permits and she goes to church on Sundays. That doesn't sound like such a bad life to me.'' She laughed. ''Matter of fact, it sounds a lot like *mine*.''

''And mine,'' Belinda agreed, feigning a sulk. ''No offense, but I'd rather have a little more excitement than that.''

''Oh? You mean like you had the other day? I heard about the food fight you had with Paul Randall.''

''No! Of course not! I don't know what came over me.'' She felt her cheeks growing uncommonly warm.

''I do,'' her grandmother offered. ''You stopped trying to be the perfect preacher's daughter for once. You let yourself go and had some good, clean fun. Right?''

Belinda's face burned with embarrassment. ''I wouldn't exactly call it clean. It was more like messy temporary insanity.'' She started to grin shyly. ''It was fun, though.''

''Good. I'd rather see that than have you wind up a bitter old woman like Pru. She has hundreds of things to be thankful for every day, yet she doesn't recognize them because she's so busy concentrating on all the real or imagined wrongs she's suffered. Drives me crazy. I declare, if she wasn't so dear to me, I'd disown her.''

Belinda's smile grew cautious. ''You aren't going to disown me, are you, Gram?''

''Not in a million years.'' Eloise chuckled and patted her granddaughter on the arm. ''You're a smart cookie. You know a blessing when you see one. I intend to stick around and watch you and your Sam walk down the aisle. You'll make a beautiful bride.''

Try as she might, Belinda couldn't visualize the doctor standing at the altar in his tuxedo, waiting for her. Oh, she could see herself as a bride and as someone's wife, someday. Just not as Sam's.

What about Paul? That wayward thought was enough to make her heart skip a beat. Then reason intervened. She and Paul had nothing in common. Not goals, not lifestyle, not even love. Especially not love. Romantic stirrings were exciting but they were no substitute for all the other elements missing from their relationship. Like trust, for instance. If she ever found out for sure that he actually had been responsible for the church fire, as she'd once so strongly suspected, there would be no way she could ever forgive him.

Unwilling to accept the logic of her conclusions, Belinda tried to imagine herself as Paul's bride, to make herself believe such an unlikely wedding could take place.

To her utter chagrin, she found she couldn't picture that scenario, either.

Belinda walked Eloise all the way out to the sidewalk and gave her a parting hug. "I'm glad you stopped by."

"Me, too. Sure you won't change your mind

about coming to lunch with us? Verleen, Mercy and I would love to have you. We're going to that new pizza place to splurge.''

"Thanks, no. I'm way behind in my work. I'll just run across the street and grab a quick sandwich at the café.''

"Okay. But you'll be missing a real treat. Not only is the pizza very good, I made Verleen promise to keep her upper plate in while we were out in public.''

Belinda giggled. "*That* should be a real plus.''

"I thought so.'' She squeezed her granddaughter's hand and turned to leave without watching where she was going. If Belinda hadn't pulled her back in time she would have crashed right into Paul Randall's chest.

Startled, Eloise gave a high-pitched gasp. "Aagh! Where did you come from?''

"Originally or recently?'' he quipped, hands outstretched to catch her if need be. "Are you all right?''

Leaning on Belinda for support and fanning herself with her open hand, she said, "Goodness, no. You scared the life out of me. I think I'm about to have the vapors!''

You're not the only one, Belinda thought. Disgusted with herself for reacting that way, she was looking forward to the day when the unexpected sight of Paul Randall didn't make her woozy.

Eloise continued to emote. "Oh, me. Oh, my.''

Amused by the older woman's theatrics, Belinda picked up on the mood and spoke more candidly than she would have otherwise. "He's had that effect on me before, too, Gram. But don't tell him. He's liable to get a swelled head."

Paul laughed. "Hey, I don't mind…as long as my new hat still fits."

"What hat? I've never seen you wear a hat."

"Actually, I seldom do," he drawled, "but a friend talked me into buying a good Stetson a couple of weeks ago and I'd hate to see that much money go to waste."

"You? Pretending to be a cowboy?" Belinda's eyebrow arched. "That I'd like to see."

"I suppose it could be arranged."

She waved her hands in front of her as if to erase the idea. "Forget it. I was only kidding."

"You could be missing out on a good thing," Paul countered. "I already had the boots."

"Isn't that a little out of character for you? What happened to your old leather-jacketed motorcycle image?"

"Ah, well… My friend assured me women like the clean-cut, Western look much better," he told her with a slight reddening of his tanned complexion. "Says it works like a charm for him."

"So, you decided to become a counterfeit cowboy, too?" Jealousy tweaked Belinda's conscience. "Pretending to be something you're not just to impress people seems terribly unfair to me." She took a breath, intending to go on with the impromptu lecture, when Eloise elbowed her in the ribs.

"Be nice, dear. You and I would rather be wearing sandals and shorts in this miserable, humid weather. Yet here we are, all decked out in heels and these wretched panty hose. Does that make us fakes?"

"Of course not." Belinda pulled a face of disgust, stressing it even more when she noticed that Paul looked highly entertained. "But I *have* to dress this way for work. Grown men don't have to play cowboy."

Laughing softly, affably, Paul said, "You've lived here so long you don't notice what's right under your nose. Do you think every man who's wearing camouflage-colored clothing and an orange cap is on his way to the woods to go hunting?" He swept his arm in a wide arc that took in the whole town square, including the courthouse in the center. "Look. You won't see more camo than this on the first day of deer season. There's no difference between that and the Western look."

He had a valid point. Sort of. People did seem to recreate themselves at will these days. Belinda was thinking about conceding when Eloise piped up. "Right. Well, I'd best be going. Verleen gets testy if she takes her antacid and then doesn't get to eat on time. Bye-bye."

Paul watched her breeze off. "I like your grandmother. She's quite a character. Is she your father's mother?''

"No. My mother's."

"I don't remember you being so close to her before."

"I wasn't." Belinda sighed, thinking. "Gram came to stay with my dad and me for a little while after Mom died. That was a mistake. She and Daddy fed off each other's grief so much that neither of them was healing. When she realized what was happening, she left us alone."

"That must have been hard on you, too."

Amazed, Belinda stared at him. "How did you know?"

He stuck his hands into the pockets of his slacks and shrugged. "Been there, done that, as they say."

"You used to tell me your mother had been gone so long you didn't even recall what she looked like."

"Well, maybe I exaggerated a little."

"You did? Why?"

"You'd lost your mother a lot more recently than I'd lost mine." His eyes were bleak for only an instant. "I didn't want to have to lie about how long it took me to get over it. I figured, if you knew the truth, you'd ask me about it and I didn't think I could explain without making things worse. Especially for you."

"That's kind of sweet…in a dumb way."

"I'm a prince among men." Paul half smiled. "So, how about lunch? You free?"

The lie almost stuck in her throat when she said, "No."

"Okay. It was just a thought."

"Sorry." Belinda wished he'd give up and go away before her galloping guilty conscience got the better of her.

"Actually, I was hoping we could set aside our differences long enough to talk about my aunts' problems over lunch. I need a woman's perspective on their crazy behavior. But if you're too busy…"

There was something about his sincere concern for others that softened her heart. She shook her head pensively. "I must be crazy to even *consider* going out to eat with you."

"At last we agree on something," Paul quipped. "So, does this mean you've changed your mind? You'll come?"

"Well… Okay. But we have to keep it short. I'm only doing this because Gram told me a very interesting story about your family this morning and I'd like to hear your version. Wait right there. I'll go get my keys so I can lock up."

Paul watched her walk away and disappear into her private office. He blew air out of his lungs with a noisy whoosh. It was getting harder and harder to maintain a casual bearing when Belinda was nearby. He'd thought his courtroom experience had made him a pretty good actor until he'd come back to

Serenity and tried to act unaffected in her presence. Choosing the right words to face a stubborn jury was nothing compared to the stress of trading light-hearted quips with her!

Disgusted with himself, he reviewed their most recent conversation. Why in the world had he told her about giving in when his friend had dared him to buy the Stetson? And if that weren't bad enough, he'd announced that the hat was supposed to help him attract women! What nonsense. He hadn't even taken it out of the box since he'd been fool enough to buy it. He exhaled another sigh. Judging by the last few minutes, his normally logical thought processes must be seriously out of whack.

Good thing he wasn't going to have to spend a lot more time around Belinda. He was already a basket case. If his illogical desire to please and impress her got much worse, there was no telling what he might say or do.

Paul shook his head, snickering at himself. He was getting too emotionally involved for his own good. His main reason for being in Serenity was to aid his aunts. Second, he wanted to prove he was innocent of any wrongdoing in the fire that had burned down the old church. Those were reasonable goals. Maybe even attainable ones.

Stepping back in time and taking up where he and Belinda had left off, however, was neither. They'd never had a chance in the first place. As a rational adult he knew that their youthful dreams of happi-

ness had been nothing more than the innocent long-
ings of two lonely kids who'd believed they were
madly in love.

Love? Paul felt his gut knot as he remembered
holding her tight and promising he'd always care.
Maybe they had once loved each other, as well as
either of them knew how. And maybe he was still
harboring some of those same tender feelings. But
that didn't mean he and Belinda were compatible
enough to build a successful future together.

Wishing wasn't enough. It never had been.

Chapter Seven

They settled on a short walk across the town square to a locally run café that advertised their daily lunch special would be served in less than fifteen minutes, or the order was free. In twenty years, the management had never failed to deliver.

Belinda's problem was forcing herself to eat once she got her food. Paul had removed his tie and rolled up his shirt sleeves, making him appear more at home in the casual surroundings. Seated across the narrow table, he was stirring a glass of iced tea and watching her intently.

She'd ordered the special, a hot roast beef sandwich, hoping that the gravy would help her swallow past the lump in her throat. If she was ever going to develop a fatal case of indigestion, this was probably the meal that would do it.

"I hate to see you have to rush so," Paul said amiably. Resting his elbows on the table, he concentrated on her. "So, you eat and I'll talk first. What was it you wanted to know about my family?"

"Ummpf." Mentally comparing Paul to the waitresses who always waited until your mouth was full before asking if the meal was satisfactory, Belinda finally managed to choke down the bite in her mouth. "Gram said both your aunts were once in love with the same man. What do you know about that?"

Paul rocked back, his brow furrowed. "Nothing. Are you sure that's what happened?"

"Pretty sure. Supposedly, Prudence fell in love with the family gardener. When Patience started flirting and won him away from her, their father blew his stack and sent the guy packing."

"Sounds about right for this town," Paul said cynically.

"It wasn't the town's fault. That was the way things were done in those days. Girls—good girls— didn't go against their fathers' wishes." Her words hung in the air between them like a heavy curtain.

Finally, Paul said, "Seems to me that practice hasn't changed much. At least not in your case. You always did what your father wanted, too."

Belinda laid aside her fork and blotted her lips with her napkin to give herself time to carefully choose a reply. Then she looked straight at Paul. "I tried to. After Mom died, I was all Daddy had left.

You didn't know him like I did. If I'd gone away with you, the way you wanted, I don't know what would have become of him. Especially after..." Her voice trailed away.

"After the fire, you mean. Go ahead. Say it. Someday, I'm going to convince you I wasn't involved. I just haven't figured out how to come up with the proof."

"It's way too late for that, and you know it," Belinda declared, which was why she couldn't quite believe he was being sincere, even though she wanted to.

Nodding, Paul soberly agreed. "Let's drop the subject. That was a bad time for everybody."

"Some good did come out of it," she said, seeking to focus their discussion on more positive aspects. "Have you ever considered what our lives might have been like if I *had* run off with you?"

"Meaning?"

"We were kids, Paul. I hadn't graduated from high school and you had no marketable skills. I doubt you'd be where you are now if you'd had me tagging along while you struggled to get an education. And I'd have been miserable, feeling guilty and worrying about abandoning my dad. You'd probably have wound up so frustrated you'd have chucked all your big plans just to try to make me happy. It was a no-win situation. For both of us."

His attitude softened. "When did you get so smart?"

"When I finally grew up and realized that our parting was all for the best. We're old enough now to look back and see that the Lord is always faithful, just like He promised, even though it's hard to understand what's going on at the time." She heaved a deep, sorrowful sigh. "I wish I could take all the kids I know, shake some sense into them and prove that *no* situation is ever hopeless."

"Sounds to me like you've tried," Paul said.

"I have." Leaning back in her chair and remembering, Belinda slowly shook her head. "One of the young people in our youth group at church recently tried to end her life because of a fleeting disappointment she would probably have laughed at a few years from now."

"Is she all right?"

"Yes, thank God—literally. But it could just as easily have ended the other way. The whole concept of kids considering suicide makes me frantic."

"And frustrated. I know what you mean."

She pushed her plate aside. "I suppose you do. You've had your share of serious setbacks to overcome, too. I really am glad to see how far you've come."

When he answered there was an underlying hostility to his tone in spite of his efforts to subdue it. "Ah, yes. My triumph over my unrefined upbringing. The kid with the jailbird father actually made it through college and law school. Imagine that. What a surprise."

Belinda's cheeks flushed. "I didn't mean it like that."

"Oh? Then how did you mean it?"

"I was trying to give you a compliment." When he seemed unmoved, she added, "You have to believe me, or..."

"Or what?" One dark eyebrow arched. "You'll start throwing food at me again? In public? You'd better not or you'll ruin your first-class reputation. I may not have to live in this town, but you do."

She could see the righteous anger draining out of Paul's expression. His dark eyes were beginning to sparkle. *Oh, thank You, God, he believes me,* Belinda prayed, rejoicing inside. Now, if she could just keep from putting her other foot in her mouth, maybe their relationship wouldn't get any more strained than it already was.

"I could always fall back on the excuse I used when Gram asked me about the food fight," Belinda said.

"Which was? Let me guess. You blamed the whole ruckus on me?"

"No! And wipe that smirk off your face. I didn't blame any of it on you. I claimed temporary insanity."

"Not a very original defense."

"Well, it's the truth." Vivid memories of the silly altercation made her grin so broadly her cheeks hurt. "But now that I think about it, you were so self-righteous and smug after you scared me into dropping that jar of sauce, it's no wonder I splashed you. You were practically asking for it.''

"Oh, really?''

"Yes, really.'' Belinda leaned forward to stare at him and reinforce her point. He didn't even blink. She, on the other hand, felt an immediate jolt of awareness as their gazes met. Her skin tingled. Her stomach churned. Her mouth went dry while her palms began to perspire. She laced her fingers together on the table to still their barely perceptible trembling and watched in awe as Paul placed his large, warm hands over them.

"I suppose it's best if we agree that I drove you to act up,'' he told her in a hushed voice. "Otherwise, word could get around that we were actually having fun, and Sam might start to think he was getting a fruitcake instead of a normal bride.''

Belinda tried to pull her hands free, but Paul held them fast, so she quit struggling rather than attract unnecessary attention. "What made you bring *that* up?''

"I just thought I should remind you of who you are. And who I am.'' *Not to mention get my own dangerous thoughts back on track,* he added to himself. "And while we're at it, how about telling me what secret project Sam has up his sleeve.''

"You're as bad as he is!''

"There's no need to insult me,'' Paul said, only half kidding.

Feeling the relaxing of his grip, Belinda slowly

withdrew her hands and placed them in her lap so she could clasp them together out of sight. "I will ask Sam to fill you in, though. His idea is really wonderful. I don't see any reason he wouldn't want to share it."

"I can," Paul said flatly. He leaned back in his chair and nodded thoughtfully. "Okay. Ask him. A few more days one way or the other won't matter. I have to go to Harrison to catch up at the office. Tell him I expect to be back at Aunt Prudence's by next Saturday at the latest."

He pulled out his wallet and handed Belinda a business card, then picked up the bill for their lunch and stood beside the table. "My secretary can take a message if I'm not in the office."

Belinda held Paul's card by its edges and stared at it for long seconds. *Look, Daddy,* she thought sadly, *you were wrong. Paul did amount to something after all. I knew it. I told you he would.*

When she looked up again, Paul had finished paying their bill and was on his way to the door. Dozens of other customers in the café were watching him leave, too. As soon as he was out of sight, everyone's attention turned to the table where Belinda sat. A few folks smiled. The rest peered at her sideways or peeked from under lowered lashes while they tried to appear uninterested.

The scenario struck her so funny she felt like climbing up onto the seat of her chair, waving her arms and announcing in a loud voice that she was *not* on a date, was *not* seeing Paul behind Sam's back and was *not* a bit interested in the handsome attorney.

Talk about more fodder for the gossip mill! A forthright denial like that would only serve to focus on her actions and increase unwarranted suspicion. Everybody was probably going to think she and Paul were an item, anyway, especially since he'd held her hands in public. If she went out of her way to deny there was anything romantic in their relationship, they'd be *positive* she was lying.

Belinda was taking a last sip of her iced tea when her breath caught in her throat and the tea slid down the wrong way. She sputtered. Gagged. Coughed into her napkin so loudly she sounded like a beached seal. And no wonder! She'd choked on a lot more than a swallow of tea. She'd choked on the truth.

In the middle of the sip, it had suddenly occurred to her that it *would* be a lie if she insisted she wasn't having any romantic thoughts in regard to Paul Randall. And not just a little lie—a real doozie!

Blushing, she jumped to her feet, hurried out the door and headed back to work.

The Chamber of Commerce office fronted on the town square and faced the brick-and-stone Fulton County courthouse. According to the engraved cornerstone, that building dated back to the eighteen hundreds. Sometimes, Belinda wished she were part of that simpler era, when time moved more slowly and life was less complicated. She was leaning on the counter, gazing out the window, when Sheila popped in with a bright, "Hi!"

"Oh, hello." Belinda straightened, stretched.

"I brought you a soda," Sheila said, handing over one of the white plastic cups she carried. "With ice. I know you don't like to drink them out of a can."

"Thanks. I can use the caffeine lift."

Sheila giggled. "No kidding. You looked like you were asleep on your feet when I got here."

"I was just daydreaming."

"About what? Hey! Were you planning how to set me up with that lawyer friend of yours, like I wanted?"

Belinda pulled a face. "Actually, no. I was imagining how peaceful things used to be, back when Serenity was first being settled."

"Peaceful? Oh, brother. You do have on rose-colored glasses, don't you? Life was *hard* back then."

Belinda mused, while she sipped her cold soda. "I suppose you're right. People did have to work more to accomplish things, unless they were wealthy and could afford lots of servants, of course."

"You mean like the Whitakers? I understand they used to be the richest folks in town. Which reminds me. You never told me how the dinner at their place went. I'll bet it was really elegant. With the right designer and enough money, that old mansion could be turned into a real showplace."

"It was a showplace, once," Belinda said. "But I'm afraid it'll never be one again."

"Why not? Whoever buys it can fix it up."

Sighing, she shook her head. "I suspect the old house is going to be demolished, instead."

"Oh, what a shame!"

"No kidding." Sipping, thinking, Belinda finished her soda and disposed of the cup. "I shouldn't say any more. Not yet. I haven't gotten Sam's permission to talk about his plans yet."

"His *permission?*" Sheila nearly choked on the notion. "Oh, pul-eeze."

"That's just common courtesy. It doesn't mean I'm not thinking for myself. Sam took me into his confidence because he trusted me, and I intend to live up to that trust."

Sheila chuckled wryly. "You know, sometimes you act like you *do* belong in another century."

"I think I'll take that as a compliment," Belinda said with an amiable smile. "Besides, the rules haven't changed in thousands of years. The Ten Commandments are still as valid as they always were."

"I suppose you're right. I don't have trouble keeping most of them, but I sure do wish the one about not coveting had been left out." She peered at Belinda. "Which brings me back to my original question...how's it going between you and Paul Randall?"

"Fine."

"Mmm, that's what I heard. Seems you and he had a hot and heavy lunch in the restaurant across the square. They say he grabbed your hands and practically held you prisoner. Is that true?"

"Of course not!"

"He never touched you?"

"I didn't say that." Belinda felt a blush warming her cheeks. "But he didn't force me to go or make me stay there. I could have left anytime I wanted."

"Uh-oh. That's what I was afraid of. You didn't want him to let go of you."

"I didn't say that, either!"

"You didn't have to. I can see it in your face. Guess I'd better find a new prospective husband for myself. It looks like you aren't going to want to share Paul."

"There's nothing to share," Belinda insisted. "We're just old friends—I mean acquaintances— who happened to eat lunch together so we could discuss his aunts." Contemplating Sheila's last observation, Belinda wrinkled her brow and pressed her lips into a thin line. "What do you mean you can see something in my face? There's nothing there to see."

"Wanna bet? Every time I mention Paul's name your eyes glass over and you look like your mind is taking a vacation."

"I do not. I can't. I mean... Oh, dear. Tell me you're kidding."

Sheila shrugged. "Sorry. No can do. I know you

too well to miss the signs. If you didn't want to hear the truth, you shouldn't have reminded me of the Ten Commandments.''

"Okay," Belinda said, squaring her shoulders and dealing with the problem in a no-nonsense fashion. "I'll accept the fact that you can see a change in me. We're both women and we're close friends, so that figures. Now, tell me, do you think it's as obvious to other people?"

"Like who? Paul?"

"No! I don't have to worry about Paul. He's never understood me. I'm talking about Sam."

"Not a chance. Sam Barryman is too busy thinking about all the ways he can make more money to notice if you get a little spacey once in awhile." She giggled. "I do think it's dumb to be seen in too many places with Paul if you're still interested in Sam, though. Some busybody is liable to carry tales."

"I'm not trying to hide anything," Belinda insisted. "There's nothing to hide."

"Then why are you worried about what Sam might think?"

That question floored Belinda. If she never intended to marry Sam, why be concerned? Simply wanting to avoid hurting his feelings was an insufficient answer. Was she still being influenced by her grandmother's advice regarding a possible future with the doctor? Perhaps. Yet there was more to her current uneasiness than that. She and Sam had been

® *Love Inspired*®

™

Steeple
Hill®

When I found these Love Inspired novels, I found hope."

— Beverly Denmark, Buffalo, N.Y.

Now it's your turn to fall in love with ❤️ *Love Inspired®*

Scratch the silver heart, complete and return the card on the right to receive 2 Love Inspired® novels.

These books have a combined cover price of $9.00 in the U.S. and $10.50 in Canada, but they are yours FREE!

> "It's a pleasure to read good, interesting, clean in thought, word and character, books."
> – Bonnie Langley, Basile, LA

> "I really LOVE these Love Inspired books. It's great to know someone thinks enough of readers to publish clean Christian books for us to read."
> – Agnes Westphal, Elmire, MI

> "I am writing to thank you for the Love Inspired series of books... We all need a little romance in our lives and this wholesome, inspirational series is exactly what I have been looking for."
> – Karen Kuehn, Warner, AB

> "I love this series. It lifts my spirits."
> — Laura Rusiecki, Nanuet, NY

SPECIAL **FREE** GIFT
We'll send you a wonderf
gift absolutley FREE - just fo
trying Love Inspired

FREE BOOKS and a **FREE** GIFT
No obligation or purchase necessary!

▶ DETACH AND MAIL CARD TODAY! ▶

Love Inspired®

Scratch off the silver
area to see what the
Steeple Hill Reader
Service has waiting
for you! ➔

YES!

Send me the **2 FREE** Love Inspired® novels.
I understand that I am under no obligation to
purchase any books as explained on the back
of this card.

303 IDL C6PZ

103 IDL C6PY
(LI-TE-01)

NAME	(PLEASE PRINT CLEARLY)

ADDRESS

APT.#	CITY

STATE/PROV.	ZIP/POSTAL CODE

Steeple Hill Reader Service™ — Here's How it Works:

Accepting your 2 free books and gift places you under no obligation to buy anything. You may keep the books and gift and return the shipping statement marked "cancel." If you do not cancel, about a month later we will send you 3 additional novels and bill you just $3.74 each in the U.S., or $3.96 each in Canada, plus 25¢ shipping & handling per book and applicable taxes if any.* That's the complete price and — compared to cover prices of $4.50 each in the U.S. and $5.25 each in Canada — it's quite a bargain! You may cancel at any time, but if you choose to continue, every month we'll send you 3 more books, which you may either purchase at the discount price or return to us and cancel your subscription.

*Terms and prices subject to change without notice. Sales tax applicable in N.Y. Canadian residents will be charged applicable provincial taxes and GST.

dating for nearly a year. Their relationship *was* in a comfortable and untroubled rut. Was it wrong to want to remain within the safety of that rut, even if she never intended to commit to him for keeps?

Sheila waved a hand in front of Belinda's eyes. "Yoo-hoo. Wake up. I asked you a question."

"About Sam," Belinda murmured. "I know. That's what I was thinking about."

"And?"

"And Sam knows how I feel. He respects my decision. As long as he doesn't start insisting that I agree to marry him, the way he used to, nothing between us needs to change."

"You mean, he's proposed and you've turned him down?"

"Don't look so shocked. Marriage is serious business. I'm not ready to make that kind of lifelong commitment."

"You were ready ten years ago, when Paul Randall was in line to be the groom."

"No," Belinda said cynically, "I only thought I was ready. Talk about naive. I figured, since I'd asked God to make my wedding happen and I was doing my best to follow all the rules in the Bible, I couldn't fail. What a shock it was when I learned *I* wasn't the one running the universe."

"Do you think you'll ever settle down with Sam?" Sheila asked softly.

Sighing and shaking her head, Belinda said, "I sure wish I knew."

"Yeah," Sheila said with a brief nervous chuckle. "I'll bet poor old Sam does, too."

Belinda waited until she figured Sam would be through seeing patients for the day, then phoned his office. His receptionist put her call through without delay.

"Hi. It's me," Belinda began. "How are you?"

"Beat. This has been one of those days. I had three emergencies before nine."

"Is everybody okay now?"

"Yes," he said with a weary sigh, "but it shows how badly we need our own hospital. I don't want anybody to suffer because I don't have access to the equipment I need to help them."

"Neither do I." Belinda had never heard Sam express such purely altruistic sentiments. Moved by his clear concern for others she asked, "Would you like to come for dinner tonight?"

"Maybe tomorrow. I didn't sleep much last night and I have a surgery scheduled for seven in the morning so I'm going to bed early." He yawned, then added, "Want to go to bed with me and keep me company?"

The man seemed to have a special knack for ridding her of any tender feelings toward him almost as soon as she acknowledged them, didn't he? "Please, Sam. Don't start."

"I know, I know, you're not that kind of girl. If I had a nickel for every time..."

Rather than let him continue in that vein, Belinda purposely interrupted. "Getting back to your plans for building a hospital. I saw Paul today. He—"

"I know you did. I even know where you had lunch."

"Good. Do you also know what we talked about?"

"Not everything."

She could sense Sam was smiling on the other end of the line. That was a good sign. "Basically, Paul wanted me to tell him what your plans were for the Whitaker property," Belinda explained.

"Did you?"

"Of course not. I wouldn't break your trust."

"At this point, I can't see that it matters much. All he'd have to do is ask Prudence, providing she remembers what we talked about. She was pretty out of it the other night."

"Only because she's so scared of change," Belinda said wisely. "The Whitaker house has become her refuge. According to Gram, the only time Miss Prudence was away from home for more than a few hours, after she turned twenty-one, was when her father was in the hospital in Little Rock. She wanted to stay close so she spent the night in the city."

"All the more reason she should support my project," Sam said. "I'll remember to mention that the next time I talk to her. In the meantime, tell Randall as much as you want. Say whatever it takes to convince him he belongs on our side. He'll be a valuable ally if the old lady refuses to listen to reason.''

"I suppose you're right.''

"As always,'' Sam quipped.

Belinda didn't feel much like trading witty remarks. Instead, she bid the doctor a simple goodnight. As she hung up the phone she closed her eyes and sighed. Sheila was right. The most important elements in Sam's world were prestige and profit. People finished a distant third.

Was Paul any different? she asked herself. His concern seemed to be for his aunts, yet his focus was on how much money they could get for their property and how best to invest it.

Which made him sensible, not nefarious. It was as big a sin to waste what the Lord had given them as it was to try to unfairly squeeze more money out of the deal. Nobody purposely went out and announced to the world, "Here I am. Cheat me.''

Picturing the naïveté of the Whitaker sisters made Belinda uneasy. In the area of high finance they seemed little more than lambs being led to the slaughter. Given free rein, Sam would try to convince them to accept his offer because of all the good they'd be doing for the town, just as he'd already told Prudence.

On the other hand, what was Paul's motive for offering his professional advice? He'd never been particularly close to either of his great-aunts until recently. Before he and his father had arrived in town ten years ago, the sisters hadn't even mentioned having a grandnephew. Her eyes widened in alarm. Maybe he wasn't related at all!

I'm getting paranoid, Belinda thought in disgust. *Why would Paul's father lie about being Whitaker kin?*

Her imagination was quick to answer, *Why not? He lied about his arson conviction until Daddy found out the truth and made a big scene.*

Remembering, she sighed and shook her head. Paul had always refused to tell her much about his early upbringing but he'd never lied about what he did disclose. She knew his mother had died while his father was in prison and he'd spent over a year in various foster homes. When his father was paroled, he'd reclaimed Paul and they'd come straight to Serenity.

The first minute Belinda had seen young Paul, she'd cared about him. He'd looked so determined, so angry, so stand-offish, so tough…and so lost. The truth had been hidden in his veiled glance but Belinda had recognized it immediately. She'd seen that same look in her own eyes plenty of times since her mother had gone home to be with the Lord.

She and Paul Randall were soul mates. It was as simple, and as complicated, as that. Belinda blinked back tears. Befriending him had been the right thing, the Christian thing, to do. Her only mistake had been in assuming that the emotional bond they'd shared was the same as the love between a husband and wife. It wasn't, of course. She knew that now.

But if her teenage tears and heartfelt prayers had been enough, the closeness she and Paul had experienced might someday have blossomed into the kind of perfect love between a man and a woman that lasted forever. The kind of love she'd seen and felt in her own home when she was growing up.

That kind of love was a special, precious gift from God.

One she'd been searching for all her adult life.

One she had yet to find.

Chapter Eight

For Belinda, the days seemed to crawl by until the weekend. On Saturday morning, she was so keyed up she decided to put on her shorts and work off her nervous energy in her garden. Snuffy was with her, running in circles and darting into the bushes to track invisible rabbits while Belinda dug out stubborn weeds from among the snapdragons by her front porch.

Paul will be back soon, she told herself over and over, immediately countering with, *it doesn't matter to me.*

Which, of course, was a fib. "I sure hope, since I'm only lying to myself, it doesn't count," she muttered, incorrectly assuming she was alone.

Eloise was close enough to overhear. "Why should you do that?"

"Oh!" Belinda jumped. "You startled me, Gram. Where did you come from?"

"I walked over. I hadn't seen you in a few days so I baked you some cookies." She held up a clear plastic baggie. "See? Your favorite."

"When it comes to your cookies, they're *all* my favorites." Smiling, Belinda got to her feet and dusted off her hands. "Cookies for breakfast sounds perfect. I haven't had anything to eat since last night. Come on in. I'll make us some coffee."

Following her to the door, Eloise asked, "Did you and Sam have a nice time at the movies last night?"

Belinda stopped in her tracks, nearly causing a collision. "How did you...? Never mind. I know. So, which branch of the Serenity grapevine tattled?"

Eloise giggled. "I heard the news from Patience. It seems she and Paul's friend Milton were sitting in the very last row of the theater. That's probably why you and Sam didn't notice them."

"Patience *Whitaker?*"

"Don't look so shocked," the older woman remarked, unconsciously primping with her free hand. "Gray hair does not mean a person's life is over."

"But...Patience?" Belinda couldn't get over the idea.

"She's a lot more likely candidate than Prudence."

"Well, *that's* true, I suppose."

"So," Eloise said with a grin and a nod toward the door, "are we going to have coffee, or not? If not, I'm going on over to Verleen's. She's always got a fresh pot brewing. Even in the summertime.''

Paul got directions from his aunts and drove past Belinda's house twice before he decided to stop. It was that or take the chance of being reported to the police by her snoopy neighbors. The ones across the street had already gathered on their porches and were staring at him as if he were a dangerous criminal.

He pulled slowly into the drive and parked. Before he could get his car door open all the way, a black, brown and white dog raced up, scrambled across his lap and landed beside him on the car seat.

Temporarily startled, Paul put out his hand so the friendly little beagle could take a sniff before he began petting it on the head. It responded by wagging its tail so hard it nearly fell off the seat. Paul steadied it. ''Whoa! Where did you come from? Huh?''

The dog spun in tight circles beside him, clearly excited and eager to have discovered a new friend.

Paul laughed. ''We're not going for a ride, if that's what you want. But I guess we'd better ask the lady who lives here where you belong so you don't run out into the street and get hurt.''

Reacting to his kindly tone of voice, the dog leaped up to try to lick his face.

Paul caught it to keep it from dancing in his lap. It scrambled and wiggled against his chest, still trying to wash his face, as he got out of the car and started toward Belinda's front door. *What a lucky break.* If he'd engineered the diversion himself, he couldn't have chosen a more useful or cooperative accomplice.

Luck has nothing to do with it, he corrected, realizing he'd fallen back into his old way of thinking. He'd been praying for an easy way to approach Belinda Carnes, and the Lord had provided it. He just hadn't expected his answer to arrive in the form of a friendly little dog.

He climbed the stairs, knocked on the metal frame of the screen door and called, "Excuse me. Anybody home?"

"Just a minute."

At the sound of Belinda's voice, the little dog's feet paddled the air so hard Paul almost dropped it. He clamped his hands around its rib cage and held it out so it wouldn't scratch a hole in his shirt. Or in him.

Belinda began to grin and shake her head when she got close enough to see Paul's dilemma. "You'd better put her down or give her to me before she runs herself to death getting nowhere," she said, laughing as she pushed the screen door open. "How did you manage to catch Snuffy in the first place? She's usually pretty shy around strangers."

"Oh?" He handed the dog over, watching the mutual joy of the reunion. "Then I suppose you won't believe she jumped into my car with me as soon as I opened the door, huh?''

"Not hardly." Lowering the energetic dog to the ground, Belinda spoke to it as if it were a child. "Gramma's here, Snuffy. Go find Gramma and tell her you want a cookie."

Paul shoved his hands in his pockets and struck a purposely casual pose as the dog dashed off. "How about me? I like cookies, too."

"Yes, but you don't live here."

"True. I did return your dog, though. Of course, I didn't know she was yours at the time, but I should still get credit for doing a good deed."

"I suppose you're right," Belinda conceded. She gave the screen door a push. "Come on in. My grandmother's visiting so the neighbors probably won't be too scandalized."

"Want me to stand out here and announce it before I come in?" Paul teased. "That lady across the street looks real worried."

"No more than usual," she said, waving to the woman past Paul's shoulder and calling, "Hi, Liz," as she ushered him in.

Snuffy returned in a whirl, sniffed Paul's shoes, then headed for the kitchen. "Just follow the dog," Belinda told him. "She's on the right track."

"What energy! If those cookies will do that for her, I'd like to order a couple of dozen for myself."

Belinda laughed gaily. "I think it's more a matter of heredity than what she eats. She's been like that ever since she was a puppy. Once she outgrew the tendency to trip over her own ears when she put her nose to the ground, she's been on the run. If I ever saw her walk anywhere, I'd figure she was sick.''

"I think she's cute," he said. "Real lovable." *Like her mistress.*

"Thanks. She seems taken with you, too. Are you sure you don't have liver treats in your pockets? Snuffy's a sucker for those.''

"Not the last time I looked." Paul chuckled. "But I'll try to pick some up before I visit the next time, just in case she doesn't remember she likes me.''

"Good idea." She swallowed hard as what he'd said registered fully. "Visit the *next* time?"

"Just making conversation," Paul replied. He sauntered into the small kitchen and greeted Eloise warmly. "Good morning. Nice to see you again. I was going to say it's nice to run into you—again, but I didn't want you to think I was making fun of our near collision at Belinda's office last week.''

"That was funny, wasn't it?" Eloise held out a plate. "Would you like a cookie? I made them myself.''

"I'd love one. Snuffy tells me they're excellent."

Belinda broke in as she handed Paul a cup of steaming coffee. "You're not going to believe this, Gram. Snuffy actually made up to Paul.''

"Well, of course she did," Eloise said, reaching

down to ruffle the little dog's silky ears. "She's a sweet little thing. Aren't you, baby?"

"But she doesn't like—" Belinda broke off in mid-sentence, leaving an unmistakable hole in their conversation.

"Who doesn't she like?" Paul asked quietly. "Sam?"

When Belinda didn't reply, her grandmother answered for her with great enthusiasm. "Of *course* she likes Sam. Everybody likes Sam."

"Maybe not everybody," Paul muttered into his cup.

Belinda felt trapped between defending Sam out of loyalty and insisting on the absolute truth. Not that her grandmother would listen to anything negative about the man she'd already decided would make a perfect grandson-in-law. At this point in the conversation, Belinda figured she'd be lucky if she could merely get away with changing the subject.

"Oh, Paul!" she blurted, louder than she'd intended. "I forgot to ask. Do you take sugar or cream in your coffee?"

"No. Black is fine."

"Okay. Um, if you change your mind…" Her heart sank when Eloise interrupted to continue with her praise of Sam.

"I've told Belinda over and over she should count her blessings that a wonderful man like Dr. Barryman is so serious about her."

Paul's eyebrows raised. "Is he." It wasn't a question.

"Oh, yes," the older woman went on. "I'm sure it's just a matter of time before they announce their engagement."

"Are you planning on baking the wedding cake?" he asked. "You really should. You're a wonder in the kitchen. That cake you made for Aunt Pru was delicious." He saluted her with the remains of a cookie. "So are these."

Eloise blushed at the compliment, then raised the cookie plate. "Thank you. Have another?"

"I don't want to eat Snuffy's share."

Giggling, Eloise said, "Don't worry. I can always bake more. I was thinking of making oatmeal-raisin this afternoon. If you like that kind, I'd be glad to do up some extras for you."

Belinda stood back and watched their conversation with amazement. In the space of a few minutes, Paul had managed not only to stop Gram's gushing over Sam, he'd also persuaded her to bake him cookies! No wonder he was so successful in court. The man was a marvel at subtle manipulation. In Belinda's view, that didn't make him sociable, the way Gram was seeing him, however. It made him risky to trust.

"So, Paul, you never said why you stopped by," Belinda interjected. "Is everything okay?"

He paused long enough to take another sip from his cup and smile casually. "As okay as it gets when both my aunts are under the same roof. I did ask Aunt Patience about the problem you and I discussed. She denies everything.''

When his glance darted toward Eloise, Belinda quickly relieved him of his nearly empty cup and took him by the arm. "Let's go out into the garden and talk about it, shall we? Gram needs to get home to make those cookies she promised us, and I wouldn't want my neighbors to think you and I were up to anything in here by ourselves.''

"I do?'' Eloise sounded confused.

Belinda smiled sweetly and nodded. "Yes, dear, you do. Paul may not be in town much longer, and you wouldn't want to disappoint him, would you?''

"Of course not. I'll get right to it.'' She breezed happily off on her mission, calling, "See you later.''

As soon as Eloise shut the door behind her, Belinda dropped Paul's arm. Her shoulders drooped. "Sorry about all that Sam business. She has a one-track mind.''

"And your happiness seems to be the track it's on. That speaks well of her devotion to you.''

"I suppose so.''

Paul had felt a jolt of pure pleasure when Belinda had taken his arm. Now that she'd let go, the loss of contact was bothering him a lot more than he liked to admit, even to himself. The confines of the small kitchen seemed to be closing in on him, urging him to step close to her again. To reach out and renew their physical connection. To take her in his

arms and kiss her, in spite of everything her grandmother had just said about her feelings for another
man.

Walk away, his conscience insisted. *Forget about
Belinda and walk away. Now. Before you do something you'll be sorry for.*

Would he be sorry? He doubted it. He might feel
guilty but he couldn't picture himself wishing he
hadn't kissed her. The notion whirled around in his
mind, sounding more and more plausible as he con-
templated it.

He stepped closer, almost without realizing he'd
moved. Belinda was looking at him, her lips slightly
parted, her eyes wide and misty. *She knows what
I'm thinking. What I want.* The wishes of their hearts
were in tune again, the way they used to be so long
ago!

If she backed away or showed any sign of resistance he'd stop, Paul told himself. He gently laid his
hands on her shoulders, felt her tremble beneath his
touch. Everything was perfect, the faint, floral fra-
grance of her hair, the openness of her expression,
the smoky blue yearning in her eyes. Paul felt as if
he were nineteen again and so much in love with
this woman he'd die if he couldn't hold her in his
arms one more time.

The idea that he should ask her permission to kiss
her flitted in and out of his mind and was quickly
dismissed as idiotic. Suppose she turned him down
simply because she thought she should? He didn't

want to put any more obstacles between them. They already had enough of those for a dozen relationships!

Belinda saw the glow of desire light Paul's gaze, sensed the runaway rush of his shallow breathing as it sped to match hers. In awe, she lifted her hands and placed them on his warm, broad chest. His heart thundered beneath her palms. Barely able to stand, she closed her eyes, lifted her chin and waited for the inevitable.

All along, Paul had assured himself he could call a halt to his irrational action any time he wished. Then Belinda had touched him, and his willpower had vanished like a wisp of smoke in a gale. His arms closed around her.

Forcing himself to move slowly, to be gentle, he pulled her to him and bent his head to prepare for the kiss, aware that she knew exactly what he was going to do and was meeting him boldly, on equal terms.

So close he could feel her warm breath on his face and see her lashes flutter, he paused for an instant to savor the experience. First he'd taste the sweetness he remembered, then deepen the kiss if Belinda seemed at all responsive. He'd make it both a last kiss and a first kiss, hello and goodbye, chaste yet innocently romantic.

It was a fine plan—in theory. The instant Paul's lips joined with hers, however, all rational thought disappeared in a mighty surge of emotion. The sweetly pliant mouth he remembered so well was responsive, all right! It was kindling a need within him that was so bright, so fiery, he had to fight to maintain any semblance of self-control. This was not the timid, repressed girl who had ridden behind him on his motorcycle and kissed him on the banks of the Strawberry River. This was a woman. A fearless woman. One who wouldn't run away from love the way she used to.

He'd known early on that his heart was in deep trouble. That was understandable, given their mutual history. This was the first inkling he'd had, however, that the *rest* of him wasn't far behind.

Belinda felt as if she were floating in a half-asleep, half-awake state. She knew her arms were wrapped around Paul's neck, and she felt his hands moving over the back of her T-shirt in a slow, sensual caress, but she couldn't be absolutely sure she wasn't dreaming. Truth to tell, she sincerely hoped she *was* dreaming. The alternative was unthinkable!

Tensing, she chanced a peek. Reality was waiting on the other side of her lowered lashes. Handsome, enticing reality. This couldn't—shouldn't—be happening. Not to her. Not now. Not here. Oh, but it felt so good, so right.

In another second I'll push him away, she assured herself, only half believing it. *Just a second or two. Maybe a minute. Maybe...* Reminded of the night Paul had first asked her to marry him, she sighed.

Maybe she shouldn't have sent their chaperone off to bake cookies. *Yeah, no kidding!*

This situation is my fault, Belinda reasoned, trying hard to focus her scattered thinking. The sensations of Paul's closeness were so overwhelming she could scarcely breath, let alone form coherent ideas. Only one thing was clear. They weren't kids anymore. If they stayed in each other's arms and kept kissing the way they were, their shared temptation was liable to sweep away the moral principles that she, at least, held dear.

That mustn't happen! She hadn't saved herself for all those years to waste her virginity on a man she'd probably never see again once his business here was concluded.

Marshaling her defenses, Belinda managed a slight resistance, hoping that would be enough to convince Paul they were making a big mistake. To her astonishment, his hold slackened. He was letting her go! Without a fight!

Filled with intense relief and remorse, she whispered the first prayer she'd thought of since Paul had swept her into his embrace, a simple, heartfelt, "Thank God."

"You should thank Him," Paul said hoarsely, his lips moving lightly against her cheek. "If I didn't know this was wrong and care what the Lord thought of me, you'd be in serious trouble, lady."

"I know." Belinda leaned away from him to look into his eyes. Latent passion still showed in his expression. No doubt Paul could see the same telltale emotion in hers. "I had no idea...." Embarrassed, she lowered her glance and stepped back.

Paul's hands slid gently down her bare arms till he could grasp her hands. "I've wanted to do that since I first walked into your office."

"You have?" Misty-eyed, she searched his face for sincerity and found it.

"Yes," he said softly, "but that's no excuse. I'm sorry. Really sorry."

What could she say? That she wasn't sorry? Perish the thought, even though it was true. No man had ever kissed her like Paul just had—not even Paul himself. It was amazing. And scary. All sorts of inappropriate notions had arisen out of that one kiss and were racing madly around the fringes of her consciousness. She'd been wrong when she assumed her prior temptation was as bad as it could get. What had happened between Paul and her ten years ago was *nothing* compared to this! Maturity definitely had its drawbacks.

Penitent, he watched her, waiting for a response. Any response. Finally he asked, "Speak to me? Please?"

And say what? she wondered. Dealing with her flood of confusing feelings was hard enough without being required to chat coherently, too.

Belinda pulled her hands from his and backed away, hoping the added distance would help her focus. It did. A little. It also let her see how truly apologetic Paul was. His broad shoulders slumped, his hair was mussed, his brow was wrinkled, his mouth was pressed into a thin line, and the muscles were twitching at the joint of his jaw.

Poor guy. He looked awful. He also looked as endearing as a lost puppy, which made Belinda glad she'd put the length of the kitchen between them. She refused to lie and say she hadn't wanted him to kiss her. Besides, that wasn't what he'd asked or what he obviously wanted to hear.

Sympathetic, she said simply, "I forgive you."

Paul's resulting smile lit up the whole room, bathing Belinda in its sweetness and making her heart skip.

"Hey, that's good news," he told her, followed by a deep, relieved sigh. "You had me worried for a minute."

When he started to take a step toward her she held up her hand like a traffic cop. "Hold it right there, mister. I said I forgave you. I didn't say I wanted to repeat the mistake we both made when we... You know."

Paul nodded and raked his fingers through his thick, dark hair. "Oh, yeah. I know, all right."

"Then you do understand my problem."

"If it's anything like mine, I sure do," he said, eyeing the back door. "Tell you what. Snuffy and I will meet you in the yard. Join us when you're ready, and we can finish our discussion outside, the way you wanted."

Temporarily at a loss, Belinda began to chuckle at her befuddlement. "I'd love to. You wouldn't happen to remember what we were talking about, would you? I don't have a clue."

Paul paused, his hand on the doorknob, and looked at her with a mischievous little-boy expression. "I think it had something to do with my family. Or maybe it was your grandma's cookies." He shrugged. "Oh, well. I'm sure we can find something to discuss once we get out in the sunshine where it's safe." *And stop thinking about what just happened between us.*

With a quiet snort of self-derision, he turned and left the room. He didn't know about Belinda, but he was *never* going to forget that kiss.

Or the woman who had shared it.

Chapter Nine

Belinda talked to herself, and to the Lord, for a few minutes before she gathered her courage, poured more coffee and went to join Paul in the back yard. He was seated on the grass under a maple tree, leaning against the stout trunk. Snuffy had crowded in next to him and was poking his hand with her nose, trying to coax him to pet her. Obviously, the dog considered Paul a part of her extended family. Belinda wished she could say the same.

"I brought you a fresh cup of coffee." She held his mug higher. "Sorry, we're out of cookies."

Paul got to his feet and brushed himself off, chancing a cautious smile as he accepted the coffee. "My loss. I guess if Snuffy can stand to be deprived, I can, too."

"I could offer you one of her dog biscuits," Belinda teased, quickly backing away. "I'm sure she wouldn't mind sharing. For some reason, she seems to be madly in love with you."

"Animals can be pretty discerning." He glanced at her over the rim of his mug as he took a sip. "You should pay attention. When Snuffy doesn't warm up to a person there's probably a good reason."

"If you're referring to Sam, forget it. The problem is, he doesn't happen to like dogs. That's all."

"Sounds like a bad sign to me," Paul said. "You were always nuts about animals."

"I can adjust." Belinda knew he was purposely needling her, trying to get her to say something negative about Sam, and she refused to take the bait.

Paul chuckled low, obviously amused.

"What are you laughing about?"

"You." He moved two lawn chairs into the shade under the maple and waited for Belinda to join him. When she didn't, he sat in one of them and continued, "In case you don't know it, you're the most stubborn, inflexible woman I've ever met. When you said you'd be able to adjust, the idea struck me funny."

"I am not stubborn!"

He gestured at the spare chair. "Oh? Then why are you standing way over there in the hot sun instead of sitting here in the shade by me? I promise I won't lay a hand on you again. Cross my heart."

What could she do? If she stood her ground, Paul

could claim he was right about her being standoffish. But he looked so good, so appealing, casually sitting there drinking coffee and petting her dog with his free hand, that she wondered if she could manage to approach without letting her mind wander to places it had no business going.

She compromised by moving the empty chair farther from his before sitting in it. "There. Happy now?"

"That's a little better," Paul said with a wry smile. "You don't have to be afraid of me, you know."

It's myself I'm afraid of, she thought cynically. "I'm not afraid of you."

"Maybe that was a bad choice of words. Nervous might be closer."

"You're getting warm," she said, blushing when she realized belatedly that that particular phrase could also have a physical meaning. "I...I mean, you do make me kind of uncomfortable."

"I can tell." Saddened, Paul thought back to the long-ago church fire and Belinda's outspoken negative reaction to him in its aftermath. Given that history, he supposed he couldn't blame her for continuing to feel uneasy, even if she couldn't pinpoint exactly why.

What he wanted to do at that moment was jump to his feet, grab her by the shoulders, look her in the eye and shout to the housetops that he was innocent. If he were still as big a fool as he'd been when it had all happened, he might have made the mistake of trying—and maybe frightened her worse, he realized with a start.

Fortunately, he was able to conceal his momentary lapse. His nonchalant facade remained firmly in place while he pondered his dilemma. Life was like a court of law. Overt emotion was no defense against false accusations. If anything, it harmed the situation. Facts were what he needed. Later, he'd drop in at the local newspaper office and see what their archives had to say about the aftermath of the fire. At this point, any clue would be a blessing.

Belinda took a deep breath and slowly sipped her coffee, finally managing to focus on something other than her current proximity to Paul. "I did speak to Sam about his project," she offered. "He said I can tell you. He's planning to build a hospital."

"Wow." Paul's eyes widened. "He doesn't think small, does he?"

"You mean you really didn't know?"

"No. Not the details. All I'd been able to find out was that some property, including my aunts' twenty-plus acres, was being considered for rezoning to commercial. I assumed Sam wanted to build apartments or a small shopping mall like the one his office is in now." Paul paused, speculating, as he shook his head slowly in disbelief. "A hospital will cost a fortune."

"I'm sure he's thought of that. He has partners, of course. And ties to a larger health system. It's a feasible plan. We've needed a facility like that in Serenity for a long time."

"That's true. I hope he can put the deal together."

"You do?"

Paul chuckled low. "Yes, Belinda, I do. I'm not a monster. All I want is a fair deal for my aunts. Don't you think they deserve to be properly compensated for a prime piece of real estate?"

"Of course, but…"

"Do you think I should be willing to lower the asking price, no matter how a reduction affects Patience and Prudence, simply because your boyfriend intends to use the property for a good cause?"

She made a face. "When you put it that way, it sounds really unfair."

"Good. It's supposed to." Paul got to his feet and handed her his half-empty cup. "I'd better be going. Tell Sam I'm still working on Aunt Prudence. I expect to have her consent to sell within the next week or so. The rest will be up to him. If he truly wants the Whitaker estate, he's going to have to pay fair market value."

"I'll tell him."

"*Only* about the property," Paul warned. "I don't think it's a good idea to mention what took place in your kitchen this morning, do you?"

Her cheeks turned crimson. "Of course not! That was just…"

"For old times' sake," he suggested with a wry smile. "Goodbye, Belinda. Have a great life."

She sat very still, watching him turn and walk away. His farewell words had been so much like the ones he'd used when he'd left town all those years before, they were causing her actual physical pain. *Have a great life,* Paul had said. Funny, she'd assumed she already was until he'd shown up in Serenity and proved otherwise.

Eloise was in the midst of baking, just as she'd promised, when Belinda dropped in. "Whew! It's a good thing you have air-conditioning, Gram." She made herself at home at the kitchen table and began to nibble warm cookie crumbs. "You'd better not do too much. Your ankle is liable to swell again if you don't rest it."

"I know." Eloise sighed. "I was only going to make those cookies for Paul. Then Verleen called. There's going to be a pie supper down at the community center tonight."

"Really? I hadn't heard a thing about it."

"It's a benefit for that poor family over on Highway Nine. The ones that got burned out a few days back. I think their name was Nichols."

"I remember now." Belinda grinned. "Their name is Penny. But you were close. Only four cents off."

"Hush," Eloise ordered good-naturedly. "You know I have a terrible memory for names. I still don't know half the folks in our church, except by their faces, and I've been a member for fifteen years.''

"True. But we've added a lot of new members lately, too. Besides, at your age you can get away with it. Between my job at the chamber and Sam's political position, I'm expected to remember everything about everybody.''

Eloise stopped mixing the sliced peaches, sugar and dry tapioca in her bowl and made a grumpy face. "What do you mean, at my age?''

"Okay, so you're a *young* grandmother. You're still a grandmother. Mine. And I'm proud of you." She gave the older woman a hug and a quick kiss on the cheek. "Tell you what. Why don't you take a break? I'll finish the pies you've started.''

"I wish you would finish what *you've* started," Eloise said, rolling her eyes toward the ceiling in a show of maternal frustration. "When are you and Sam going to stop dragging your feet and get married?''

"Who says you don't remember things?" Belinda quipped. "It seems to me your memory's been working overtime on that particular subject.''

"I just want you to be happy." Handing over the bowl and spoon, Eloise sank wearily into the nearest chair. "I've been married and I've been single. Believe me, married is much, much better.''

"Only if you're married to the right man.''

"That's what I've been trying to *tell* you. If you

play too hard to get, Sam may find somebody else. Then where will you be?''

Where, indeed? The thought of being dumped by Sam Barryman made Belinda feel oddly content. The sensation was similar to the peace she usually sensed when she knew she was doing God's will. *How strange.* Not that she could rely on her emotions to behave in a rational manner, given what had happened that morning. Still, maybe the Lord was trying to use Paul's kiss to open her eyes.

She began to flour the board so she could roll out the first bottom crust. ''As you always say, Gram, if the good Lord wants something to happen, it will.''

''Providing we don't come along and mess up His plans.''

''Or try to help Him too much instead of trusting in His leading?'' Belinda added astutely. ''Of course, you wouldn't know anything about doing that, would you?''

''At least I recognize a good thing when I see it.''

''So do I. Believe me, so do I.'' Inwardly, Belinda mocked herself for immediately picturing Paul. What was good for one kind of woman, however, wasn't necessarily good for any other kind. She and Paul had grown apart. Far apart. No amount of wishing or praying could change that. They couldn't spend the rest of their lives standing in her kitchen and kissing passionately, no matter how wonderful it had been. There was a lot more to life, to happiness, than that, like it or not. It was easy to admit she definitely did *not* like it.

"Hey!" Eloise shouted. "Not so thin. What do you think you're making? A pizza?"

"Oops." Belinda looked at the enormous circle of dough. Even the best cook could never successfully lift that flimsy a crust into a pie plate. She started to gather it up and squeeze it into a ball. "Sorry. Guess I was daydreaming. I'll roll it out again."

"If you do, you'll take it to the benefit with *your* name on it. That crust'll be as tough as shoe leather."

"Fine. I'd like to have a pie to donate. If nobody bids on it I'll buy it back myself."

Eloise bumped her aside with her hip and commandeered the rolling pin. "You may have to. Wrap that ruined dough in waxed paper and refrigerate it until I'm through with my pies. I'll save you enough for a bottom crust. You can use your overworked pastry to make a lattice top."

"Yes, ma'am." Belinda watched her grandmother's capable hands fly into action.

The older woman threw a handful of dry flour onto the table, spread it around with her hand and kept working while she talked. "You were daydreaming about Sam, I hope."

"I have been thinking of Sam and me," Belinda conceded, "but I doubt you're going to like what I've decided."

Eloise stopped rolling and turned to stare. "You aren't thinking of breaking up with him?!"

"Actually, I was. It's not fair to keep seeing Sam when I don't love him."

"Of course you do. You just refuse to admit it." She grimaced. "It's that Paul Randall, isn't it? You've got some crazy idea you still love him, even after what he did to your poor father. Shame on you, Belinda Carnes."

"Paul said he's planning to prove to me that he didn't start the fire. He sounded very convincing."

"If he's so blasted innocent, why did he run away?"

"Well, because…" Belinda had no ready excuse.

"See? You don't know. That's because you aren't sure what the real truth is, either." Raising her eyebrows, she peered at Belinda and added, "The apple never falls very far from the tree, as they say."

"Fine. I blamed him without any proof, so why shouldn't you. But tell me this, Gram, if you really believe Paul is so evil, why are you baking him cookies?"

Eloise went back to her pie crust, rolling with a vengeance. "Christian charity."

"Phooey." Belinda paced across the room and back. "I know you. If you honestly believed Paul was guilty, you wouldn't even speak to him, let alone give him cookies."

"I would so."

"Good," Belinda drawled knowingly, "then I

can count on you to take a peace offering out to the flatlander who bought the Beasley place, then sued the pants off the city when they ordered him to clean it up. Right?''

The look of dismay and astonishment on her grandmother's face was so comical Belinda almost laughed out loud. Nodding with perception she said, ''Uh-huh. That's what I thought.''

The pie supper at the community center was scheduled to begin at seven that night. Belinda decided to go early so she could help set up the folding chairs. One whole wall was taken up by long tables of donated baked goods for the pie auction. Household goods and clothing intended for the family's personal use were stacked on the floor beneath the tables. Some of the things were new. Others were whatever the giver could spare.

The room filled up quickly. Mr. and Mrs. Penny sat in the front row with their three children, accepting hugs of condolence and sniffling with gratitude for the bounty they were about to receive. Belinda had added her own offering, as well as Eloise's, to the table of baked goods and was choosing a chair for herself when Sam breezed in.

''Sorry I'm late,'' he said. ''The Barlow kid cut his toe. They called me at home and I had to meet them at my office so I could stitch him up and give him a tetanus booster.''

"You're not late," Belinda assured him. "We haven't started yet."

"I know. I'm the auctioneer."

Surprised, she glanced around the room. Many of the usual volunteer auctioneers were present. "Why you?"

"Probably because this benefit was my idea," he said, boasting. "It was the perfect opportunity to announce my plans for a hospital, especially if I was the one in charge. So I made sure I was." He cocked his head toward the crowd and spoke quietly. "Look. Half the town is here, and they're all in a charitable mood. The atmosphere couldn't be better."

"You didn't do this for the burned-out family?"

Sam shrugged it off. "Of course I did. If I hadn't thought of it, somebody else would have. They always do. I just didn't see any reason to waste a good stroke of luck so I made a few calls and got the ball rolling."

"I see." And she did see. Sam Barryman might be a great doctor and a successful businessman, but his priorities and his sense of divine guidance were seriously flawed. Where she saw the hand of God, Sam gave all the credit to luck, instead. She sighed. His present attitude was just one more confirmation that her decision was the right one. She and Sam would never be happy together. Their motivations were simply too different.

He patted her arm. "Have a seat and watch the

master at work, honey. I'll bet we raise more money tonight than we ever have before.''

"I hope so." She managed a smile as she watched him make his way down the center aisle, stopping along the way to shake hands and greet people as if he were running for political office. Truth to tell, he had already done a lot of good for Serenity. Business was booming. And if he was successful in getting a hospital built, the benefits to the town would be enormous.

But at what cost? She'd seen Miss Patience arrive with store-bought baked goods, as usual. There was no sign of her twin sister, however, which wasn't surprising, since Prudence usually avoided crowds. What would that poor old woman do if she no longer had her house as her sanctuary? And what would become of all those cats she doted on as if they were her children? No wonder she'd been so adamant about not selling.

"Oh, Father," she whispered. "I think I see what You've been trying to tell me."

The pieces of the puzzle began to slide into place in her mind. People's happiness was more important than monetary gain. One look at the crowd gathered together to comfort and support a family in need proved that. Some of the folks who were giving most freely had little to offer, yet they'd come because they cared about each other.

Belinda cared, too. Poor Miss Prudence deserved to stay in her house for as long as she wanted to and was able to care for herself. Like it or not, Sam was going to have to find another suitable piece of property for his hospital, and Belinda intended to tell him so. Soon.

She smiled in spite of the seriousness of her decision. When she'd decided to break up with Sam the path was being prepared for her, just like the Bible promised. It was a good thing. The minute she openly sided with Prudence, Sam was going to be absolutely furious.

At that point, breaking up was probably going to sound like a real good idea to him, too.

Since it was customary to bid way too much for the pies and other baked goods, then serve them to everyone in attendance as soon as the sale concluded, Sam opened the auction with a short spiel about his plans for the new hospital. Then he got down to the business at hand.

An hour later he was almost finished auctioning everything on the baked goods table. He raised the last pie in the air, balancing it on the flat of his palm to display it. "Here we go, folks. Don't give up on me yet. We've got one more to sell before we eat."

Eyeing the slightly lopsided pie with undisguised skepticism, he drawled, "Looks like peach. Don't know who made this poor little thing, but that doesn't really matter, does it? This is all for a good cause. What am I bid?"

Silence reigned. Belinda had no trouble recognizing her amateur effort. In a community where many women still prided themselves on their expertise in the kitchen, her lack of culinary skill was something of an embarrassment.

"How about two dollars? Do I hear two?" Sam asked, chuckling.

Belinda raised her hand and called out, "Five."

A few curious people turned to look at her. From the back of the room a burly farmer hollered, "She ought to know what it's worth. That's one she brought." An undercurrent of laughter began to ripple through the crowd.

If Belinda had thought she could successfully crawl under her folding chair and hide from everybody, she would have tried to do it. Masking her hurt feelings, she managed to smile at Sam and catch his eye long enough to say, "It is peach."

Jockeying the pie plate, he grinned at her. "In that case, I bid ten dollars myself. Going once, going twice…"

"Fifty dollars!"

Every head swiveled, especially Belinda's, even though she'd recognized the new bidder's deep voice the moment she'd heard it. Paul Randall was standing in the back of the room, feet braced apart, arms folded across his chest, visibly defying his rival to up the bid.

"I have fifty." Sam's voice lacked its former enthusiasm. "I'll make it fifty-five. Do I hear sixty?"

Without hesitation Paul shouted, "Seventy-five."

Belinda wasn't the only one who gasped. All eyes snapped to Sam, waiting to see what he'd do. If that hadn't been her pie on the auction block, Belinda would have found the whole scenario pretty funny.

Gritting his teeth, Sam countered, "Eighty."

"One hundred dollars," Paul shouted. Before Sam could respond, he doubled his own offer. "On second thought, make that *two* hundred."

The wooden gavel cracked down on the speaker's stand. Belinda didn't hear Sam say, "Sold," because the meeting hall was echoing with so much cheering and loud applause.

Belinda had volunteered to help Verleen and some of the other women dish up the food, so she reported for duty right after Paul won the bidding war for her pie.

"That was some sale," Verleen said. "I never seen a peach pie that looked quite like that last one. Guess you should of made a bunch of 'em."

Belinda stifled a giggle. "No kidding. Gram gave me her leftover fixings after she finished making four pies of her own."

The older woman squinted at the crowd. "Is Eloise here? I didn't see her."

"No. The poor thing was dead on her feet by the time the last pie came out of the oven. Her ankle was bothering her a lot, too, so I talked her into staying home. It's hard to get her to take it easy, though. Lying around is not in her nature."

"Nor mine. I s'pose Dr. Sam would've slapped Eloise in that hospital of his if it'd been built already."

Her attitude gave Belinda pause. "You don't sound as thrilled about it as I thought you'd be. We do need a place like that, you know."

"That don't make it fun to visit." Verleen continued to section the spice cake in front of her. "Glad you brought Eloise's pies for her, though. Every dollar helps. We did pretty good tonight."

"I'll say."

"Did you see May Penny cryin'? She was real touched. Must a blowed her nose a hundred times."

Nodding, Belinda busied herself putting slices of cake and pie onto small paper plates while people crowded around, hoping to get a taste of their favorite.

She was so preoccupied with trying to satisfy the demand, she didn't look at who she was serving until a familiar voice asked, "Do you suppose I can get a piece of the one I bought? I've never eaten two-hundred-dollar pie before. I'd kind of like to see what it tastes like."

His genial smile took her breath away. "Paul. Hi."

"Hi, yourself. How come you didn't tell me about this benefit when I saw you this morning? I almost missed the bidding."

Belinda shot a sidelong glance at Verleen, happy to note she was chattering away with her cronies instead of paying attention to Paul. "I didn't know about it then. These benefits are usually planned in advance, but this one's for a family that was recently burned out. They needed a lot of help right away."

"So, it came up on the spur of the moment?"

"Yes." She tried to hand him some dessert. "Here. Try this one. Gram made it."

"Like I said, I'm waiting for a piece of the one you made."

"You may be sorry."

"I'll take my chances," Paul said, noting that Sam was wending his way through the crowd, heading straight for Belinda. "Just give me my pie and I'll stop bothering you."

"You're not..." When she felt an arm slip around her waist she tensed and jerked so badly she nearly dropped the thin paper plate and its contents. "Sam! You scared me."

"Did I? I guess you must have been thinking about something else, huh?"

Belinda didn't like the way Sam was glaring at Paul—or the way Paul was returning a similar look—so she thrust the plate into Sam's free hand to occupy it, then snatched up an identical piece and handed it to Paul. He thanked her politely and turned away.

Sam stayed, so Belinda found something for him to do besides glare at Paul's retreating figure. "We're about to run out of plastic forks, Sam.

Would you mind getting another case out of the storage cupboard?''

She saw him continuing to concentrate on what was going on across the room and followed his line of sight. It looked as if Paul was preparing to leave!

Apparently Sam thought so, too, because he stopped acting like he was guarding her and went to do as she'd asked. Saving her deep sigh until he was out of hearing range, Belinda finally let it go with a whoosh. ''Oh, boy.''

Beside her again, Verleen cackled. ''If them two was boys instead of grown men, they'd be mixin' it up out behind the barn, honey, instead of throwin' their money around to impress you. You'd best pick one and stick to him before they both run off.''

''I can't,'' Belinda said with a disgusted pout. ''Neither one of them is right for me.''

''According to Eloise...''

Belinda interrupted. ''I know what Gram thinks. She's told me often enough.''

''So?''

''So, she's wrong. I'm sure of that now. There's no way I'd ever be able to convince myself to marry Sam.''

''What about the other one?'' Her already wrinkled brow creased in thought. ''Hey. Wait a minute. Was he the kid who burned down your daddy's church? He was, wasn't he? Lots of folks said he'd been seen hangin' around, kind of like he was casing the place, just before the fire.''

"Paul was there to see *me*," Belinda said with conviction. "That's why he came back that night. He was worried about me."

"That so? Then why'd he take off afterward and hightail it out of town like he did?"

Sobering, Belinda shook her head. "Gram asked me the same question. I suppose that's partly my fault. There was so much confusion, and I was so worried about what might happen to Daddy, I'm afraid I accused Paul of being responsible, too."

"Makes sense. He probably did it."

"No. No, I don't think so anymore."

"Eloise tells me he had plenty of good reason to be mad at your daddy, that's a fact." She snorted. "Yes, sir."

Belinda opened her mouth to contradict, then shut it again without speaking.

Nodding solemnly, Verleen said, "Sometimes it's best to let sleeping dogs lie, you know. 'Specially if you've been bit by that particular one before."

Chapter Ten

The following Sunday morning was going to be the day Belinda came right out and told Sam she could never marry him. She'd thought it all through. It would be easy to steer their conversation in that direction while he drove her home after church.

By ten-thirty, however, she was still standing on her front porch, waiting and wondering if she was going to get the chance. She allowed him fifteen more minutes, then hopped into her car and raced toward church.

"Please, Lord, just get me there on time and I promise I'll never speed again," she muttered. "You know how I hate to be late."

Which is a personal problem, she countered. *God is not responsible for my quirks.* Penitent, she retracted her earlier prayer and lightened up on the gas. "Sorry, Father. I know better. I should be thankful I'm able to go at all. If I'm late, it'll be Sam's fault, not mine. Or Yours. I'll just sneak in the back door and grab the first seat I see so I don't disturb the service."

Unless Paul Randall is nearby, she added to herself. In that case, she might have to walk the aisle, even if that did call undue attention to her tardiness. It was better to be a little embarrassed in front of her friends than to wind up forced to sit too close to Paul again.

Then why go at all? a voice within her asked.

Because I belong in church, Belinda answered. Nothing said she couldn't visit a different church once in awhile, though. She brightened. What a wonderful idea! Miss Prudence's little church was right on her way. Instead of passing it, she could stop there with time to spare. The plan was perfect. She'd been wanting to talk to Prudence, anyway, and apparently the Lord had used Sam's tardiness to send her in the right direction. What a blessing!

Rejoicing, Belinda wheeled into the unpaved parking area surrounding the one-room church. Cars and trucks all faced the sanctuary, radiating out like spokes of a wheel, with the white-painted church as the hub. Spiritually, it *was* the hub, she thought, happy she'd decided to stop.

Grinning at the prospect of worshiping here, she hurried to the open door and was greeted warmly by an elderly gentleman she suspected was the pastor.

His grip was firm and sure, his eyes brimming with love. "Good morning! We're so glad to have you with us."

"Thank you," Belinda said. She peered past his shoulder. "Is Miss Prudence Whitaker here? I understand this is her church."

"It most certainly is." Stepping aside, he gestured. "She always sits right up front. First row. We can't afford a sound system like the bigger churches have, and she can hear better from up there. Please. Go on in. I'm sure she'll be proud to see you."

"I hope so." Considering her prior support of Sam's plans to develop the Whitaker estate, she wasn't quite sure what Prudence's reaction would be when she showed up.

Starting down the aisle, Belinda began to picture herself as one of the kids in Miss Whitaker's old fourth-grade class, being called up to the teacher's desk for correction. She lowered her gaze and watched the toes of her shoes moving along the hardwood floor, just as she had when she'd been Prudence's student years ago. *How funny!* Although she hadn't reminisced about those days in a long time, her subconscious apparently still hid a gut-level desire to please her former teacher.

Smiling at the absurdity of her reaction, Belinda reached the front of the church. Prudence was there, as promised. The fold-down wooden seats looked like they had once belonged in an ancient movie theater. There were two empty spaces between Prudence and the center aisle.

"Miss Prudence?" Belinda asked quietly. "Are these seats taken?"

"Why...no." She brightened immediately and turned slightly to better face Belinda. "What a lovely surprise! Is your grandmother with you?"

"No. Sorry." Belinda took the seat closest to her former teacher. "I was running late this morning, and it seemed like the Lord was telling me to stop here as I drove by, so I did."

"How sweet." Prudence patted her hand. "And how interesting."

"Isn't it! I love it when stuff like this happens. Which reminds me. We need to talk after church. I've been thinking, if you want to stay in your house, you have a perfect right to. All we have to do is figure out how to make it feasible." She saw tears begin to glisten in the old woman's blue eyes.

"What a lovely thought," Prudence said softly.

One more empty chair remained between Belinda and the aisle. She was sitting sideways with her back to it when someone reached past her to hand Prudence a well-worn Bible.

Crowded, Belinda straightened in the narrow seat. "I'm sorry, I..." Her mouth dropped open, then slammed shut. "You! What are you doing here?"

"Bringing my aunt the Bible she left in the car," Paul said gruffly, "and going to church." One eyebrow arched. "What are *you* doing here?"

"I was passing by and..."

Prudence leaned forward to speak quietly to her nephew. "Belinda couldn't have ulterior motives, dear. We came in my station wagon, not your car. Remember? So she couldn't have known you were here." She sat back, cupped her hand around her mouth and whispered to Belinda, "Don't worry about him. He's been a grump ever since Sister talked him into letting her borrow his new car again this morning." She giggled. "And besides, I suspect you scare him a bit."

"Me?" Belinda started to glance at Paul, then changed her mind. "I do?"

The older woman nodded, offering no further explanation. Sitting primly in her seat, she opened her hymnal as a pianist began to play an introduction.

In the confines of the narrow seats, Paul's shoulder butted against Belinda's, and she couldn't help feeling the warmth of his arm radiating through the sleeve of his suit coat. If there had been any extra room she would have scooted farther away, for her sake as well as for his. Unfortunately, the seats were all fastened together, so distancing herself wasn't an option.

Droplets of perspiration distracted her as they started to trickle down the back of her neck. She blotted her forehead. A sound system wasn't the only thing this sanctuary lacked. It also had no air-conditioning. If it hadn't been for the ceiling fans, the place would have felt like an oven by the time the service was over. It already reminded her of a rain forest, humid and close.

She wished she could slip off her short jacket without bumping into Paul's arm. She wished she'd worn something cooler. She wished she could sneak away and remove her sticking panty hose before she cooked in them.

And that wasn't the half of it. Belinda grimaced. She sure wished she'd known Paul was going to be here. And she wished Sam had picked her up on time, the way he always did. She also wished she'd had sense enough to keep on driving instead of stopping at the tiny church when she felt the urge! Any of those things would have helped her avoid this predicament.

What a mess! There she was, a captive of good manners and her strict upbringing, sandwiched in next to the one man who only had to look at her to hopelessly muddle her thoughts. If she got up and left now, Miss Prudence would be embarrassed in front of her whole church family, not to mention what an impolite action like that would do to Belinda's already overworked conscience.

You're supposed to find peace in church, she told herself, confident that God would provide for her needs as soon as she surrendered and let Him take over. *Oh, please, Lord?* she prayed silently. Things couldn't possibly get worse than they already were, so it stood to reason they had to get better.

Slowly accepting that logical conclusion, Belinda

was starting to relax when the congregation got up to sing. She looked right and left. Hymnbooks were apparently as scarce here as everything else. Prudence was already sharing hers with two women on her opposite side.

Singing the first verse of the old hymn from memory, Belinda faltered on the second and felt a gentle nudge to her right. Paul held out his hymnal, wordlessly offering to share. She grasped her half of it out of habit, realizing too late what a revealing mistake she'd made. Her hands were shaking so badly the pages wiggled!

Paul cradled her hands beneath the book and steadied them. His touch was sure and gentle. It should have had a calming effect. It didn't.

Before the third verse ended Belinda was feeling so light-headed she began to wonder if she'd get away with blaming her weakness on the high air temperature if she fainted dead away!

By the end of the service most of the women were fanning themselves vigorously. The men sat there and sweated, stoic as usual. When the final amen came, Belinda was relieved to note that everybody else seemed as eager to get out of the sweltering church as she was.

Prudence took her arm and started up the aisle. "Maybe it's my age, but every summer seems hotter to me."

"It was very warm this morning," Belinda

agreed. "I'm spoiled. My church has air-conditioning."

"I know. So does Sister's. But a little place like this can't afford that kind of thing."

Paul was walking directly behind them. "They could if someone gave them an endowment," he said. "You could do that, you know, if you agreed to sell the estate."

"But I don't want to leave the house Father built." She tightened her hold on Belinda's arm. "You don't know how sick it makes me to even think of selling. Belinda understands. Don't you, dear?"

"Of course I do." She shot a quick, warning glance over her shoulder at Paul, then focused on her elderly companion, speaking sympathetically. "There has to be some way you can keep your place." Behind her, she heard Paul's derisive snort, so she added, "Well, there does. All we have to do is put our heads together and think of it."

Prudence was blinking rapidly, her eyes moist. "Will you join us for Sunday dinner? Please?"

"I don't know, I..." She would have begged off if Paul hadn't butted in.

"I'm sure Ms. Carnes has other plans, Aunt Prudence."

Belinda managed a calm, self-possessed smile and said, "Actually, I don't. Sam stood me up this morning. I suppose he had some kind of medical emergency that he had to take care of."

"Then you'll come with us!" Prudence almost jumped up and down with joy. "You and I haven't had a chance for a nice chat in years. I want to hear all about your ideas for my house."

"I haven't worked anything out yet."

"That's all right. You will. You always were a bright child. So eager and well-behaved."

Belinda was basking in the praise when Paul spoiled it. "This isn't elementary school, Aunt Pru. And you don't have your father's money to keep that house going anymore."

That was a surprise to Belinda. "You don't?" She looked at Paul. "They don't?"

"No, they don't," he said flatly. "Between Patience's extravagances and Prudence's philanthropy, they're broke. If it weren't for their pensions and social security, they'd starve to death."

"It's not that bad," the older woman insisted. "The good Lord provides for our needs. He always has and He always will."

Belinda saw Paul roll his eyes and sigh. She, too, believed that God was faithful, but she also knew that He expected His children to take good care of whatever He'd given them. If the sisters had wasted their inheritance, it was doubtful they could count on God to bail them out.

Sensitive to Prudence's mood, she kept that opinion to herself and pointed to her white car. "I'll follow you. Where are we going to eat?" If looks could have killed, she'd have been pushing up daisies, thanks to the icy glower Paul sent her way. Apparently, when he'd bid her that final-sounding goodbye and told her to have a great life, he'd meant it to be *very* final.

"The Linden's buffet over in East Serenity is about the only place open on Sunday," Prudence explained. "We thought we'd try it out. I hear it's very good."

"Fine. I'll meet you there." She began to back away. "If I'm late, go ahead and start without me."

"I wonder why she thinks she might be late?" Prudence mused. "We're all leaving here at the same time."

Paul held the passenger door for his aunt, watching Belinda make her way to her car. "I suspect she wants to go check on the doctor first."

"Of course she does. Why didn't I think of that?"

Paul slammed the door and circled the station wagon, muttering to himself, "I wish *I* hadn't."

Belinda dashed home to change clothes, make sure Snuffy had plenty of cool drinking water and check her answering machine for recent messages. There were a few seconds of semi-incoherent babbling from Sheila, but Sam hadn't called, which meant that he must still be involved with a patient. While she was changing, she sent up a quick prayer for his success and the health of whomever he was working on. In less than ten minutes she was on her way to the restaurant.

From the outside, Linden's looked like the normal coffee shop it once had been, but the interior now contained an enormous buffet. Belinda hadn't eaten there very often in the past year or so because Sam didn't like the noise of all the diners or the task of dishing up his own meal. She paid the cashier at the door, glad she'd decided to arrive alone rather than make Paul feel obligated to buy her dinner. At this point, the less she owed him, the better.

The after-church crowd had filled nearly every seat. If Paul hadn't been taller than average she might have had trouble spotting the secluded booth he and his aunt occupied.

Arriving a bit breathless, Belinda tossed her purse onto the bench beside Prudence. "Whew! I've never seen the place this full."

When Paul started to stand, she waved him down. "Sit. Eat. I'll go fill a plate and be right back."

"I wish I'd gone home and changed, too," Prudence observed. "She looks so refreshed."

"Yeah, I see that," Paul grumbled. He'd shed his suit coat and tie and rolled up his shirt sleeves, but he still didn't feel nearly as cool and collected as Belinda looked. She'd put on a yellow sundress with tiny shoulder straps and pulled her dark auburn hair back with a matching ribbon. Her cheeks were flushed, the way they'd looked right after he'd kissed her, and her eyes sparkled like sunlight on rippling water. The result was so awesome he had trouble forcing himself to stop staring.

By the time she returned, he'd managed to regain a semblance of self-control and go back to his meal. "So, did you find Sam?" Paul asked as she scooted into the booth next to Prudence.

"Sam? No, why?"

"I thought that might be why you were delayed."

Belinda laughed softly. "Nope. All I wanted to do was go home and get out of my hot outfit. Sam's a big boy. He can take care of himself. He doesn't need me."

"Does *he* know that?" Paul asked with an enigmatic grin.

"I doubt it. Sam is a nice guy, but he has a little trouble listening to any ideas other than his own." She smiled at Prudence. "As you already know."

The elderly woman made a sour face. "I certainly do. If I'd been younger, or stronger, I'd have grabbed that confounded needle of his and given him a taste of his own medicine right in the—!"

"Aunt Pru!" Paul leaned across the table toward her and placed a finger to his lips. "Hush. If you get upset again you'll have everybody thinking Sam was right to give you that sedative."

"That's okay," Belinda countered, seeking to lighten the mood, "if they haul you off and lock you up, I'll bake you a cake with a file in it so you can escape."

Glad for a diversion, Paul took up the challenge of wits. "I don't know that I'd count on that plan, Aunt Pru. I know what her cooking is like. If I were a jailer, I'd immediately suspect that anything that crudely made had to be a ruse.'' To his delight, Belinda's eyes widened in disbelief, then narrowed with indignation.

''Oh, yeah? What makes *you* such an expert?''

Pleased, Paul smirked. ''I've been eating all my life.''

''No kidding? Well, if you're referring to the pie I made for the benefit last night, I'll have you know that it earned the most money on record.''

''No doubt. I remember that part vividly.'' Watching her cheeks reddening, he decided he'd better stop teasing. ''Sorry. I couldn't resist. Your pie actually tasted very good, judging by the sliver I managed to get of it.''

''Shame on you,'' Prudence scolded. ''Belinda was just trying to cheer me up.''

''So was I.'' He concentrated on carving the slice of ham on his plate. ''What we really need to do is focus all this wasted brainpower on a solution to your problems.''

''I think Sam should find a different piece of land,'' Belinda offered. ''Then Miss Prudence could keep her house.''

''For awhile,'' Paul agreed. ''Trouble is, the place is falling apart and there's no money to properly repair it. Before long, it won't be worth saving.''

''Sam doesn't intend to save it.'' Laying down her fork, Belinda blotted her mouth on a paper napkin.

"Are you sure about that?" Paul saw her nod.

A quiet sniffle from Prudence drew their attention. "That house is special to me because Father built it. I wouldn't mind so much if I thought the place would survive even if I moved away. I'm afraid my old house is too much of a dinosaur, though, just like Sister and me."

Belinda disagreed. "It should be a national treasure." She sat very still as the idea formed. "Like a historical monument! It was the first estate in this county, maybe this whole end of the state. Paul? What do you think?"

Mulling over her suggestion, he finally shook his head. "That won't help. Even if we do convince some organization to step in and preserve the house, that still doesn't give Aunt Pru any place else to live. If she doesn't sell, she won't have the money to resettle."

Disappointed, Belinda conceded he was right. However, something else, something tenuous, kept trying to gel in the back of her mind. How could the sisters sell the house and preserve it at the same time? Who would be nuts enough or philanthropic enough to pay for it, then turn around and give it back? Certainly not Sam. Unless...

A clever plan was beginning to take shape in Belinda's mind. If she could present her idea with enough emphasis on personal gain and community prestige, there just might be a chance Sam would go for it.

Paul stood. "I'm going to go get some dessert. Can I bring you ladies something?"

"I'll have cheesecake, please," Prudence said.

Belinda said, "Me, too. Thanks." Waiting until Paul had left the table, she told her elderly companion, "I don't want to get your hopes up but I have an idea how you can keep your house from being destroyed and still get enough money to buy yourself another nice place to live."

"How?"

"I'm going to suggest that Sam buy the entire estate, just like he'd planned, then deed the residence back to the state as a historical site. There's plenty of room on the rest of the property for his hospital, and I'll bet he can claim the gift of the old house as a whopping tax deduction."

Misty-eyed, Prudence grasped her hand, squeezing hard. "Oh, dear. Do you really think that will work?"

"I hope so," Belinda said. "I'm just glad I thought of it before I broke up with Sam and made him too mad to listen to me."

"Broke up? You're not going to marry him like Eloise thought?" The old woman's gaze drifted across the room to the crowded buffet table where her grandnephew waited in line for their dessert. "Does that mean you've decided to marry Paul?"

"No!" Belinda blurted, attracting the attention of a few nearby diners. She lowered her voice. "No. I could never let myself get serious about him."

"Why not?" Drawing a shaky breath, Prudence answered her own question. "Oh, my. It's because of that awful fire, isn't it? You still blame Paul."

"Not exactly," Belinda said, hedging. "I don't want to suspect him. The trouble is, I'll never know for sure what happened that night, and as long as there's any doubt I'll have to keep dealing with it. I can't forget. I've tried."

Prudence pressed her fingertips to her lips and began to weep silently. Finally she lowered her hands and said, "Paul didn't do it. I *know* he didn't."

"It's sweet of you to believe in him," Belinda told her, "but I'm afraid you're prejudiced."

"No! You don't understand. I know Paul didn't set that fire because I was there!" she whispered hoarsely. "The whole thing was my fault!"

Belinda tensed. "What are you talking about?"

"It was an accident," the old woman said between sniffles and halting breaths. "I didn't mean to do it." Prudence's bony fingers were tearing her napkin to shreds in her lap. "Promise you won't tell? Promise?"

So shocked she could hardly think, Belinda nodded woodenly. "What happened?" Flabbergasted, she stared at her elderly companion. Did she dare believe what she'd just heard? Or was the surprising confession merely a fib designed to clear the way for Paul? Speaking of which...

Belinda's head snapped around. Paul was turning

from the dessert table with three small plates in his hands. There was no way she could sit here and waste time making polite conversation when what she wanted to do was take her former teacher by the shoulders and shake her until she spilled the whole story.

Grabbing Prudence's hand, she slid out of the booth and ordered her to do the same. "Come on."

"Where are we going?"

"To the ladies' room. Where we can talk privately."

"What about Paul?"

"He's the reason we can't stay at the table." Belinda was clearly growing angry. "And I'm not about to wait for a better time. Ten years of blaming the wrong man for a crime he didn't commit is quite long enough, thank you."

She had to force herself to slow her pace so Prudence could keep up. Fortunately, they had the rest room to themselves when they entered. Belinda whirled. "Okay. Let's have it. How did you start the fire? And this had better be good."

"It…it was a candle," Prudence managed to say between shuddering sobs. "I lit it when I went to the church that night to meet Eldon."

"Eldon Lafferty? I thought he was long gone."

"Everybody did. But he wrote to Sister all the time. I recognized his handwriting on the envelopes."

This scenario was so bizarre it was beginning to sound almost plausible. "If Miss Patience knew where he was, why didn't she say something to somebody? Why let everybody think he'd disappeared?''

"Because Sister never got her letters," Prudence said with a shaky intake of breath. "I kept them for myself."

Belinda was losing patience at the convoluted telling of the tale. "Okay. Get to the point. What does that have to do with the fire in Daddy's church?"

"I told you. I was meeting Eldon there." She reached for a paper towel to blot her tears. "I took a candle with me to put in the window because that was the secret signal we'd arranged."

"This is unbelievable," Belinda said. "Why didn't you just turn on the lights?"

"Because I didn't want to make anybody suspicious. Besides, I thought if I kept the light real dim, Eldon wouldn't know it was me instead of Sister until I'd had a chance to explain, to tell him how much I still loved him. But he recognized me right away. We had a terrible row. I forgot all about my candle until much later, when I heard the sirens." She burst into renewed weeping. "I should have known it was a sin to sneak around that way. But I was so lonely. And I'd missed him so much."

Overcome by the portent of everything she'd learned, Belinda sagged against the rest room sink. "I understand that part. I just don't know why you never spoke up."

"I couldn't! What would people think? And what

was the use? Paul was long gone, and nobody was ever arrested.''

''You have to tell him,'' Belinda insisted.

''I can't! He's like the son I never had.''

''All the more reason you owe it to him.'' She straightened, her chin high, her mind made up. ''I'll give you until tomorrow morning. If you don't tell him the truth by then, *I* will.''

Leaving Prudence behind to wash off her tears and pull herself together, Belinda started to return to the table where Paul waited. She'd thought she could bluff her way through the rest of the meal, but the moment she saw him, her stomach did a flip-flop and her resolve vanished.

Totally confused, she couldn't decide whether she loved him the way she used to, or hated him for running away from trouble when she'd needed his moral support so badly. Only one thing was certain, there was no way she could sit across a table from that man and make polite conversation without him being aware that something important had changed between them. The best thing to do was make a hasty exit.

Paul started to rise as she approached. ''Where's Aunt Prudence?''

''In the ladies' room. She'll be back in a jiffy.'' Belinda retrieved her purse. ''I have to be going.''

His abrupt ''no'' took her by surprise.

She quickly recovered, waving gaily as she turned to make her escape. ''Sorry. Can't be helped. Bye.''

"No. Wait! Eat your dessert," he called after her.

Belinda ignored him. Almost to the door, she heard another familiar voice that brought her up short. It sounded like Sam's! Puzzled, she paused long enough to glance at the nearby tables. It *was* Sam. And he was with another woman!

Belinda faltered, her eyes widening in disbelief as the woman looked up. Sheila? Her so-called best friend?

Irate, Belinda stomped over to their table and concentrated all her pent-up irritation on Sam. "What are *you* doing here?"

Sam leaned to look past her with a scowl. "I could ask you the same question. I saw you sitting over there with Randall."

"Leave him out of this. Where were you this morning? I had to leave for church without you."

"Had to? Or *wanted* to?" Sam asked. "I was only a couple of minutes late. You could have waited."

"You're *never* late. You told me so when you were giving me tips on punctuality. Remember?" She turned to her friend. "And as for you…"

"I tried to phone you first," Sheila insisted. "I left a message on your answering machine. Honest. Play it. You'll see."

In the back of her muddled mind Belinda did recall fast-forwarding through a confusing message from Sheila. Any other time she'd have been quick to acknowledge it. Right now, however, it was all she could do to keep from shouting.

Paul chose that instant to step behind her and explain. "I noticed the doctor was here. That was why I wanted you to stay at our table and eat your dessert." He made a token effort to take her arm. "Are you okay?"

"No. I am *not* okay," Belinda said angrily, jerking out of his grasp and stomping toward the exit. "Everything is a mess, especially me."

Paul followed. "Oh, I don't know. You look pretty good from here."

"Ha!" She straight-armed the door and plunged through. She wanted so badly to break her promise and tell him all about the candle that she had to grit her teeth to keep from doing it. In self-defense, she concentrated on her seething anger, instead. She was mad at everybody—Prudence, Sam, Sheila and Paul, not to mention being furious at herself for assuming the church fire had to have been caused by arson simply because that was what everyone else had believed.

"Can I take you home?" Paul asked quietly. "I don't think you should drive when you're so upset."

"I'm fine. I'm not upset," Belinda insisted.

"Then let me go get Aunt Prudence and we'll at least follow you."

Belinda had no intention of waiting for Paul to coax his weeping aunt out of the rest room. When he turned and entered the restaurant, she made a dash for her car and sped away.

Chapter Eleven

By the time Belinda got home, Sheila had left another message on her answering machine. This time, it was easier to tell what she was saying. Penitent, Belinda immediately returned the call.

"Oh, thank goodness, it's you!" Sheila burst out. "When you walked up to that table and got so mad I thought for sure you'd hate me forever."

"It's…"

"I know. It's inexcusable to go out with Sam and not tell you, only I didn't have the chance. He just showed up. I mean, we didn't have a date or anything. And by that time you weren't home. I know. I tried to phone you before I said I'd go anywhere with him. You'd told me you weren't serious about him, so…" She began to cry. "I'm so sorry."

"Whoa. I'm sorry, too. You caught me at a bad

time, and I overreacted. I shouldn't have taken my frustrations out on you. I'd already made up my mind to stop seeing Sam, anyway.''

Sheila sniffled. "You had? You're not just saying that to make me feel better?''

"I *do* want it to make you feel better,'' Belinda said, feeling lower than something that had just crawled out from under a wet, slimy rock, "because it's the absolute truth.''

"Did you decide that on account of Paul? I about fell out of my chair when he walked up and grabbed you.''

"There you go, assuming things again. He did *not* grab me.'' Cradling the receiver, Belinda slipped off her shoes and plopped into a chair. Snuffy rolled over at her feet for her customary tummy rub, and Belinda rested her feet against the dog's ribs, wiggling her toes for Snuffy's pleasure.

"Well, he tried to,'' Sheila said. "What was going on, anyway? When he hustled Miss Prudence out of the restaurant she looked like she'd been crying.''

"She had.'' Belinda sighed deeply, resolutely. "I should be able to tell you all about what happened in a few days. I just can't say anything yet. It's really a miracle.''

"A miracle? What happened?'' Sheila giggled. "I know, I know. You can't tell me.''

"Right.''

"What about Sam? Can you tell him? I sure hope

so, because he was livid after you left. I kind of liked him, though, in spite of that. If you're not interested in him anymore, I just might be.''

"Go for it," Belinda urged. "You're a lot more worldly and well-traveled than I am, so maybe it will work out between you and Sam. I'm way too small-town for him. He doesn't understand the way I think. Or the things that are important to me."

Sheila's voice quivered as she asked, "You're sure you don't mind?"

"Not one bit." Their conversation had driven home the correctness of her earlier decision. "The next time I see Sam I'm going to tell him, as gently as possible, that he and I are totally wrong for each other."

"What if he gets mad again?"

Belinda chuckled. "I'd rather he got mad now than married me and found out the hard way that we could never be happy together."

"I guess you're right," Sheila said with a sigh. "Well, good luck. You'll need it. Talk to you later. I've gotta go blow my nose."

Hanging up, Belinda closed her eyes, folded her hands and turned her thoughts to God. *It's not luck I need, Father. It's divine guidance. I'm lost. I don't know what to ask You or how to ask it. How can I possibly keep Prudence's secret when it's already done so much damage? And how can I explain my feelings to Sam without hurting him or alienating him forever? And then there's Paul. What in the world am I going to do about him?*

There was no audible answer, no rushing of a mighty wind, no lightning bolt from heaven. Surrendering, Belinda let her heart continue the prayer wordlessly.

When she finally said amen, she had received a portion of the peace she so desperately sought.

Paul had tried all the way home to get his aunt to tell him what was bothering her. Several times she'd started to say something, then stopped.

Finally, he lost patience with her. "Whatever it is that's bugging you, I'm not going to drag it out of you," he said flatly. "If you don't want to confide in me, fine. Just stop crying every time you look at me, okay?"

"I can't," she wailed.

"Then either tell me or I'm leaving this house. Now."

"You'll hate me. Belinda already does. I know it."

Paul's heart began to beat faster. "What does this have to do with Belinda? Why should we both hate you?" He held his breath, waiting. "Well?"

When the elderly woman began to talk, there was no stopping her. She related the whole sordid story, going all the way back to her girlhood and the rivalry with her sister over the man they'd both loved. Paul managed to hold his tongue until she got to the part about accidentally starting the fire with a candle. Then he exploded with rage.

"All this time you kept quiet and let everybody think I did it? How could you do that? *How?*"

Weeping, Prudence managed to say, "I didn't mean any harm."

"Harm? You don't know half the harm you've done."

"I'll…I'll make it up to you, Paul. Somehow, I'll make it up to you. I promise I will."

His fists were clenched. The muscles in his jaw were twitching. "You bet you will, madam. Starting today."

"What are you going to do?" Prudence was wringing her hands and trembling visibly.

"I'm going to take your station wagon and go collect certain people so you can tell them the story you just told me," he informed her. "And the details had better be the same the second time around because I'm not going to let you hide behind your lies again. Got that?"

"Yes, Paul."

"Good. I'm glad we understand each other. Stay here and wait for me. I'll be back as soon as I can."

Eloise was in the back seat of the station wagon when Paul pulled up in front of Belinda's house and honked the horn instead of getting out.

The instant Belinda opened the door to see what

was going on, Snuffy dashed out, barking wildly, to challenge their unexpected visitors.

Paul had the driver's window rolled down, and his bent arm was resting in the opening. He didn't smile when he spoke to Belinda. "Put the dog back in the house and get in the car."

"I beg your pardon?" Belinda looked at his other passenger. "Gram? What's going on?"

"Beats me, honey. All I know is we're going to the Whitakers'. Paul says Prudence needs me. Don't dawdle. I want to get over there as fast as I can."

"I'll grab my sandals."

"You don't need shoes," Paul said gruffly. "Just an open mind, which should be a brand-new concept for you."

Belinda's heart was racing, her pulse pounding a painful cadence in her temples as she shut Snuffy in the house, slid her feet into her sandals and hurried to the car. Was this the news she'd been waiting for? Could Miss Prudence have told him the truth already? Judging by his mood, the chances were good that she had. In which case, there was really nothing to worry about.

She chose to climb in next to her grandmother instead of sitting up front with Paul. "It'll be okay, Gram," Belinda said quietly, trying to reassure her. "I'm positive everything will be all right."

Reving the engine, Paul snorted derisively. "Things will *never* be all right around here. That shouldn't surprise me. They never have been good in this narrow-minded little burg anyway, so why should I expect an improvement?''

By the time Paul finished his quest, he had collected Belinda, Eloise and Patience, whom he found having a long, intimate picnic lunch with Milton Boggs. Rather than relinquish his date, Milton had insisted on coming along. Paul had seen no reason to deny his request. Although Boggs was anything but impartial, it wouldn't hurt to include a spectator who had not been involved in the original fiasco.

Paul whipped his carload of witnesses into the Whitaker driveway, slid the station wagon to a stop and got out. "Okay. Everybody into the parlor. This won't take long."

Lagging, Belinda tried to catch his eye, intending to smile and let him know she sympathized. Rather than look at her as she'd hoped, however, Paul took the front steps two at a time and flung open the door as if he expected everyone else to follow without question, which they did.

By the time they reached the parlor, Paul had placed Prudence in a side chair in the center of the room and was hovering over her as if she were a hardened criminal.

"Sit down. All of you," he said to the others, waving his arm in the direction of the settee and sofa. "You're the jury."

"Then we're about eight people short," Belinda ventured bravely. It was obvious that Paul was so enraged he was overreacting, and she hoped to distract him enough to give him time to calm down. "Want me to run out and round up a few more folks?"

The angry glower he sent her way was enough to deter her completely. "Okay, okay. I'll sit," she said glumly, plunking down next to her grandmother.

Eloise leaned closer to whisper, "What's going on here?"

"You'll find out. Just be patient."

"But... Poor Pru looks awful."

"That doesn't surprise me much," Belinda conceded. Folding her arms across her chest, she settled back and waited for the mock trial to begin. It didn't take long.

Paul dispensed with the swearing in of the defendant and went straight to interrogating his aunt. "I want you to tell us, in your own words, who started the fire in the church ten years ago."

"I did."

Belinda heard Patience gasp and felt Eloise tense on the sofa beside her. *So far, so good.*

"And why did you do that?" Paul asked.

"It was an accident." Prudence dabbed at her misty eyes with a wadded-up hanky. "I didn't mean to do it."

"What were you doing in that church in the middle of the night in the first place?"

Prudence looked at him, her eyes pleading for mercy. "Do I have to say?"

"Yes. You do. We all deserve to hear it."

She lowered her gaze to her lap where she was nervously twisting the hanky. "I was meeting Eldon Lafferty."

Patience's resulting squeal sounded like a mouse with the croup. When Belinda looked around, Milton Boggs was patting the old woman's hands and whispering words of comfort.

Paul pressed on. "How did you know Mr. Lafferty would be there that night?"

"Because I'd arranged to meet him. Only he didn't know it was me. He thought he was meeting Sister."

"That's a lie!" Patience shrieked, shoving Milton aside so she could glare at her sister. "I haven't heard from that man for over fifty years."

"Yes, you have," Paul said, turning to face her. "Aunt Pru has a bunch of love letters that she stole before you ever saw them. Most of them were written right after Lafferty left town. A few are more recent."

"Letters to *me?*" Patience's tone was shrill, incredulous. "You mean Eldon wrote to me, just like he promised? How do you know?"

"Because I saw the letters myself," Paul said. "She had them hidden in a box she kept under her bed." He pointed toward a side table where an old tin strongbox sat at the edge of a white crocheted doily. "They're right there, if you want to see them.

Right now, though, I suggest we all pay close attention to the rest of this story.''

Patience fell silent, leaning on Milton's shoulder and gripping his arm for moral and physical support, as Paul continued to question the other twin. ''What did you do when you got to the church that night?''

''I—I lit a candle and put it in the window of the church kitchen as a signal to Eldon, just like I'd promised. I was going to blow out the flame as soon as he got there, so he wouldn't see who it was, but my plan didn't work. Even after all those years he knew the difference between me and Sister.'' She sniffled, then continued. ''He was furious. He started yelling and throwing things. I ran out of there as fast as I could.''

Paul's voice deepened. ''What happened to your candle?''

''I don't know. I swear I don't! I suppose it might have gotten knocked over or something. I forgot all about it until much later when I heard that the church was on fire.''

''Or maybe Lafferty was so mad he started the fire on purpose,'' Paul ventured, glowering at her.

Prudence buried her face in her hands and began to weep. ''I honestly don't know.''

''Is that why you kept quiet and let me take the blame? Were you protecting your so-called lover?'' Paul asked, hovering at the edge of self-control.

''No! I couldn't tell anybody what I'd done.'' She sobbed, trembling, her eyes pleading for forgiveness. "I didn't dare. What would people think of me? What would Sister think?"

Empathetic, Belinda interrupted before he could go on. "Okay, Paul, you don't have to be so hard on her. We've heard enough. What she did was horrible, but it's over."

"Horrible?" he repeated, whirling to confront her. "It wasn't nearly as horrible as what you did to me. At least Aunt Pru was acting out of love."

"And I *wasn't?*" Belinda jumped to her feet. "How dare you say that. I befriended you when nobody else would. I even lied to my father so I could sneak away to spend more time with you."

"Ah, but in the long run, you never really trusted me, did you?"

"What chance did you give me? You never stood up and defended yourself. You just ran like a scared rabbit when things got difficult. What was I supposed to think? What was *anybody* supposed to think?"

"Anybody who had loved me would have stood by me, no matter what," Paul said soberly.

"And if you had loved me, you'd have written, or called, or something. But no, you took off and left me behind to believe the worst."

"That was *your* choice, Belinda," he said with a knowing nod. "You could have come with me. I certainly asked you to often enough."

"And you could have stayed in Serenity."

"No. That's one thing you were right about when

we discussed it the other day. There was nothing for me here.''

I was here, she thought, fighting tears of loss and frustration. *I was here.*

Acting quickly, before she lost control completely, broke down and gave away her true emotions, Belinda squared her shoulders and walked boldly out of the room, chin held high.

Paul let her go. In the background, both his aunts were crying. Milton was comforting Patience, and Eloise had her arms around Prudence.

The only person in the room without a visible comforter was Paul. Thankfully, he knew he wasn't alone. As always, the Lord was with him.

Thinking over what had just happened, Paul shook his head and sighed deeply. Finding out the truth had been the answer to his most fervent prayers, yet the resulting revelations had not healed the old wounds the way he'd imagined they would. If anything, he felt worse.

Belinda walked the four blocks from the Whitaker estate to her house as fast as she could, looking over her shoulder every time she heard an approaching car. If Paul chased after her she was going to flatly refuse to accept a ride home. No way was she going to get into any car with that man ever again. No, sir.

To her chagrin, the problem never came up. No one followed her. By the time she reached her house she was wringing wet with perspiration.

She'd always found that physical exertion was the best antidote for stress, so she slipped out of the damp yellow dress, donned lightweight work clothes, fastened her hair up with a big plastic spring-hinged clip and headed for the yard to take the rest of her aggressions out on garden weeds.

Fresh from a mad dash around the perimeter of the yard, Snuffy found a cool patch of shade and flopped down in it, panting heavily. Belinda was happy to have such uncritical companionship. "What's the matter, girl? Is it too hot out here for you?" She gave a stubborn weed a hard yank, shook the dirt off its roots and tossed it aside.

The little beagle's tail thumped in response to her indulgent tone. "You're smart to relax, baby. Smarter than I am." Belinda swiped the back of her hand across her brow to push aside her damp bangs without getting her face dirty. "At least you have short hair. Good thing you're not a collie, huh?" Rapid panting made the dog look like she was grinning in response to Belinda's silly comment.

On her hands and knees, Belinda leaned forward and reached for a clump of chickweed, accidentally connecting with a hidden sprig of puncture vine at the same time. That set her back on her heels in a big hurry. "Ow, ow, ow!"

Snuffy jumped into action, plunging into the flower bed in search of whatever had hurt her favorite human. Examining her hand through the layer of dirt, Belinda stopped worrying about her throbbing finger long enough to shout, "No! It's okay, girl. Come here. I'm fine."

Only she wasn't fine, was she? A painful sticker was only the most recent thorn in her flesh. Everybody else's life seemed to be getting better, while Belinda's fell apart. It looked like Paul was going to be able to negotiate a fair price for the Whitaker property, especially once she presented her brilliant tax scheme to Sam. Prudence was going to be able to afford a new place for herself and her gazillions of cats, plus, Lord willing, she was going to live long enough to see the family home restored to its former grandeur. Sam was going to be able to build his hospital just where he wanted it while looking like a philanthropist. And Sheila was happily exploring the possibilities of someday becoming a rich doctor's wife. Patience was a winner, too. She was going to be able to travel the way she'd always wanted, and it looked like she wasn't going to have to do it alone, either, thanks to her blossoming friendship with widower Milton Boggs.

The beagle chose that moment to crowd into Belinda's lap and lunge up to lick her face. "And I have you, don't I," she said, lovingly hugging her little dog. "You might not be a very good conversationalist, but you stick with me, which is more than I can say for some people I know."

Sensitive to her melancholy mood, Snuffy quieted and went back to her favorite shady spot to lie down. Belinda knew the dog had more sense than she did, at least with regard to the afternoon heat, but if she quit weeding and went inside to rest she'd have way too much time to think. To feel sorry for herself. Which was a ridiculous, unacceptable response to the blessings the good Lord had bestowed upon others.

Determined to banish her negative thoughts before she quit gardening, Belinda got on her hands and knees again and leaned under the spent peony bushes to get at the farthest weeds. She was so preoccupied with her emotional involvement in other people's lives and the continuing throbbing of her injured finger, she failed to hear a car come to a stop in the driveway.

The first inkling she had that something was amiss was when she felt Snuffy scampering back and forth across her bare calves and whining for attention. "Ouch. Stop that. Your nails are sharp!"

"Funny," a masculine voice mocked. "I had a manicure last week."

"Paul! What are you doing here?" Belinda rose too quickly. Her springy hair clip snagged on the stems of the peony bush. Instinctively, she pulled away. Instead of providing freedom, that only poked more branches into her hair, leaving her snared in a hopeless tangle of dead leaves and twigs. Worse, she suddenly imagined she felt the tickling of insects on the back of her neck.

"I was taking your grandmother home. She insisted we stop by on the way to check on you. Besides, I needed to apologize for losing my temper earlier.''

At that moment, Belinda was more interested in the presence of her most loyal supporter than in Paul's penitence. ''Gram? Are you there?'' she shouted. ''Help! Get me out of here!''

Paul answered instead. ''Eloise is waiting in the car. Her sore ankle has started to bother her again. What are you doing under there in the first place?''

''Weeding.'' *As if he couldn't tell.*

''You never heard of doing it with a hoe?''

''You don't have to be sarcastic,'' she grumbled. ''Are you going to just stand there or are you going to help me?''

''I'll see what I can do.''

''Hurry. I'm getting itchy!'' She felt the side of his leg brush against her waist, then saw his shoe on the ground beside her. It was one of those fancy leather loafers. Probably Italian. And no doubt expensive, she thought with disdain. There she was, wearing old, tattered clothing, her hands caked with dirt and her hair doing a good imitation of an abandoned bird's nest, while Paul remained utterly refined, as usual. When he'd changed his image from wild teen on a motorcycle to professional man, he'd certainly done a thorough job.

''Stop wiggling,'' he ordered. ''I'm almost done.''

Belinda didn't think she'd moved a muscle. ''You

try holding still with bugs crawling down your neck and see how well *you* do.''

''No, thanks.'' Paul stepped away, holding part of the bush out of her way. ''There. See if you can back up.''

Relieved, she crawled out of the trap and staggered to her feet, immediately edging away from him. Clearly, he thought her plight was comical. His lips were twitching in a suppressed grin, and his eyes were sparkling with wit.

''What's so funny?''

''You are.'' He eyed her critically.

''I wasn't expecting company,'' Belinda offered in her own defense, dusting her hands off on her already grubby shorts.

''Let's hope not. So, have you talked to Sam lately?''

''Not since the restaurant. Why?''

''I phoned him a few minutes ago. He bought your idea about turning the Whitaker house into a historical site.''

''What about his hospital? Is he going to put it somewhere else?''

''No. He won't have to. He'll split off the one lot with the old house on it, just like you suggested to Aunt Pru, and save even more money than you figured because he won't have to pay to have it demolished, either.''

''Oh, good. Then everybody will be a winner, just like I'd hoped. I was afraid Sam would be really hardheaded, especially if he knew I'd come up with the idea.''

Paul made a nonverbal noise that sounded like, "Humpf," then smiled. "He probably would have been, if he'd guessed. Which is why I let him think it was *my* idea."

"You what?''

"I said, I let him think it was my idea. Is that a problem for you?''

"Yes. No." She grimaced. "I guess not.''

"Good. We should have the whole deal put together in a few days.''

She knew what that meant. "So, you'll be leaving?''

"As fast as I can," Paul said soberly. "I can't wait to get away from this town.''

"Do you hate it that much?''

"More.''

Shading her eyes with one hand, Belinda squinted at Paul. "I'm sorry. About everything.''

He shrugged as he turned to leave. "Yeah. Me, too.''

Chapter Twelve

Belinda kept to herself, brooding, for the rest of the day. By evening she was no closer to deciding why she felt so out of sorts. Prudence's confession had provided a direct answer to her prayers about Paul's innocence, so why was she feeling so miserable? So bereft?

"Because finding out the truth didn't make any difference," she finally admitted. "Paul still hates Serenity and he's still leaving." She knew she was going to miss him more than ever now that she'd met the man he'd become. And been kissed by that man. Boy, had she been kissed! The memory of being in his arms was so vivid it made her tremble.

She plopped on the couch, picked up the newspaper and turned to the television schedule. The little beagle rolled over at her feet, begging for more tummy rubs. Belinda obliged. "Well, here we are," she said cynically. "Just you and me, Snuffy. Another exciting evening in paradise, parked in front of the TV set till we nod off. Whoop-de-do."

Snuffy's tail thumped. "Yeah, I know," Belinda said. "I don't feel like just sitting here, either, but I'm not going to let you go outside and chase wild bunnies. You might actually catch one someday, and then I'd feel terrible. Besides, it's almost dark."

Sighing, Belinda got to her feet and paced across the room to the bank of windows above the alcove in her dining room. Outside, fireflies had begun their evening courting ritual. That reminded her of Paul. Of course, so did everything else. To be awake, to breathe, was to think of him. If she had to remain in the house with nothing to do but rehash the things she should have said, the things she should have done, she'd be climbing the walls or swinging from the rafters in another hour.

She decided to leave Snuffy inside for safekeeping and go outside to water her drooping Shasta daisies and refill the dog's water bucket. The tasks weren't a necessity as much as they were a diversion, one she desperately needed.

Belinda was concentrating on keeping the trigger sprayer on the hose nozzle depressed just enough to provide a fine mist for the flowers when she noticed a black Lexus parked across the street.

Speaking of thinking of Paul all the time! Unfortunately, the car couldn't be his. Judging by his morose mood the last time she'd bid him goodbye, she didn't expect him to ever return.

She frowned. Then whose black car was it? In a county where the pickup truck was practically the official vehicle, there weren't a lot of luxury cars of any kind, let alone another one that looked like that. And besides, why would a strange car be parked in her neighborhood?

The hair on the back of her neck prickled. Uneasy, she stopped watering and held her breath to listen to the sounds of the night. A whippoorwill called. Somewhere far off, hounds were baying at the moon. Belinda felt a sudden jolt of apprehension. Either she had another bug crawling down her shirt or something in the surrounding atmosphere was making her strangely nervous.

Even small towns had their share of crime, she reminded herself, although it had been months since anything serious had happened anywhere near Serenity. Still, it was getting pretty dark, and she was out here all by herself. The one time she might need them to watch out for her welfare, there was no sign of her nosy neighbors.

A dry stick cracked behind her. Her grip on the spray nozzle tightened. Wheeling, she aimed and fired!

Paul howled like he'd been shot, which frightened Belinda even more and prolonged her counterattack. In the long seconds before she realized she hadn't been in danger in the first place, he was drenched.

Finally, she released the trigger. "Oops."

"*Oops?* Is that all you have to say for yourself?"

"Well, you don't have to get huffy. You shouldn't have been sneaking up on me in the dark like that. You scared me silly."

"I wasn't sneaking up on you," he insisted. "I was walking around the yard looking for you. I knocked on the front door, but Snuffy was the only one who answered."

"I never heard her barking."

"Are you saying you don't believe me? I thought we'd settled all that nonsense this afternoon." He brushed at his soggy shirtfront and shook the drops of water off his hands, mumbling to himself. "This shirt was silk. If I'd known you were going to attack me again I'd have worn the one with the spaghetti sauce stains."

"What did you come back for?" Belinda asked.

"Hey, I'm glad to see you, too."

She blushed, embarrassed at the unfriendly tone of her question. "Let me rephrase that. Hello, Paul. Nice to see you. What brings you here tonight?"

"I forgot something."

"Like what?"

"To ask you a favor. I meant to do it when I stopped by to apologize this afternoon. I want us all to keep Aunt Prudence's secret. Her reputation means a lot to her, and I figure mine is already trashed, so why stir up old sins?"

Belinda was both relieved and happy. "You mean you aren't mad at her anymore? You forgive her?"

"I'm working on it," Paul said with a frown. Looking at his shirt, he added, "If I'd dreamed you'd be this unhappy to see me, I'd have phoned instead."

"I didn't squirt you on purpose," she insisted.

"Oh, yeah? Then why didn't you stop when you realized it was me? It's not *that* dark out here."

Belinda's righteous indignation rose. "I did stop."

"Right. You just have really slow reflexes for your age. That's how I got this wet." Keeping an eye on her, Paul bent, turned the valve and shut off the water supply to her makeshift weapon.

"*Now* who's not being trusting?" she demanded.

"Me." Gaze steady, movements purposeful, he straightened with the dog's water bucket in hand, holding it by its wire handle. "Fortunately, I found something to defend myself with."

"Now, Paul..." Still clutching the hose, Belinda began to back away as he walked toward her with the sloshing bucket. She heard another car approaching. It stopped in her driveway. Judging by the familiar sound of the engine, it was Sam's Camaro.

"Sam! Over here," Belinda called. "I need your help."

"What the..." The doctor's choice of a colorful exclamation was *not* one she approved of.

"Go turn the hose on for me. Hurry!" she shouted.

Bracing for the surge of water, she fully expected him to comply. Instead, he came up behind her and peered at her as if she were demented. Shocked, she spun halfway around. "Sam! The water!"

That was all the diversion Paul needed. He drew back and let fly, launching the entire contents of the bucket in one mighty throw.

Belinda saw a flash of movement and a glimmer of reflected moonlight out of the corner of her eye. Acting purely on instinct, she ducked. Most of the water sailed right over her head.

She let out a high-pitched shriek, then gasped and started to howl with laughter. Paul's drenching assault had caught Sam full in the face! He was sputtering like an inept diver coming up for air after a hard belly flop.

Belinda couldn't decide which man looked the most astonished, the aggressor or his accidental victim. She always got giddy when she was overtired or stressed out, but her ensuing attack of the giggles was worse than usual. The expression on Sam's face was the most hilarious thing she'd ever seen!

Laughing so hard she was doubled over, she fought to catch her breath. Tears rolled down her cheeks. If she lived to be older than Paul's maiden aunts, she doubted she'd ever see anything this funny again.

Paul was the first to recover from the mishap. He put down the empty bucket and approached Sam with his hand extended in implied friendship. "Sorry about that, Doc. My target ducked," he said affably.

Though she was still laughing too hard to speak, Belinda did manage to punch him lightly in the ribs. Sadly, Sam was not taking their mock altercation nearly as well as Paul. Of course, Paul wasn't the one who'd been drowned in warm, greenish dog water, either. She'd scrubbed all the algae out of Snuffy's bucket a few days ago, but it had apparently grown brackish quickly, thanks to the hot weather.

Sam took a handkerchief from his pocket and wiped his face as he glowered at her. "Do you have any idea how inappropriately you're behaving?"

She'd just about regained the power of speech when his overbearing attitude started her giggles all over again. The most she could manage was, "Uh-huh."

"This won't do, Belinda. I have a professional image to maintain in this town."

"Uh..."

"I can't have you playing kid games with some delinquent from your past. Is that understood?"

"Uh..." She gasped for breath. "I... I...don't think you and I are...right for each other, Sam." He looked so flabbergasted she added, "I've been trying to tell you that for *ages*."

"You're overwrought. You don't mean it."

Belinda had laughed so hard her cheeks hurt. Taking a deep, settling breath, she cast the doctor a sympathetic look. "I do mean it. It's over between us, Sam. You'll make a great husband for some lucky woman someday, it's just not going to be me."

Brow furrowed, Sam looked from her to Paul and back again. "I see."

"No, you *don't* see," Belinda insisted. "This isn't about Paul. It's about us. You and I fell into our relationship because it was convenient. We never were right for each other."

Paul was just getting a handle on his emotional reaction to her vow that her personal problems had nothing to do with him when she decided to elaborate.

"You and Paul have the same problem, Sam. You both want me to be something I'm not. You're looking for a woman who can be a polished, refined doctor's wife, and he needs someone who loves living in the city and can fit into the new image he's created for himself. I don't belong in *either* role."

"You could if you'd try," Sam argued.

"I'm not a chameleon. I'm a person. This is the way God made me."

Chin jutting out proudly, Belinda looked both masterful and ready to cry. Paul stiffened, ready to intercede if necessary, when Sam grasped her by the shoulders, held her fast and said, "That's utter nonsense. People change all the time."

"Only if they *want* to!" Jerking free, she backed

out of reach, bumped into Paul's chest and whirled around, gesturing wildly. "Ask him. He's done it. He's *nothing* like the guy I used to love."

Totally frustrated and suddenly bone weary, Belinda threw her hands in the air, gawked at the two men and shouted, "Aaaah! I give up. You're both hopeless." Pushing past Paul, she grabbed the business end of the hose and stalked toward the faucet. "Anybody who's not out of here by the time I turn this water on is going to get soaked. Got that?"

"I'm certainly not going to stick around," Sam declared, heading for his car. "She's crazy."

Belinda watched him go, then shifted her focus to Paul. "Well? Are you going to stand there and get wet or be smart and join him?"

"Neither." Slowly he began to advance.

"Don't do it," she warned. "I meant what I said."

"I don't doubt it." He'd almost reached her.

Belinda gritted her teeth and took aim. "Don't make me do this."

"I'm not going to *make* you do anything." Moving so fast his hands were a blur, Paul deflected the hose and grasped both her wrists at the same time, pushing them behind her back and holding them there. That eliminated the danger of his being squirted. It also brought Belinda's body too close for comfort.

Caught tightly against him, she froze, barely breathing. Paul was coping pretty successfully with the emotional impact of her nearness until she tilted her head back and looked directly into his eyes.

That was enough to obliterate what was left of his self-control. No matter what she said about him, what she thought of him, there was no doubt she wanted him to kiss her. He *knew* it. From his heart all the way to his befuddled mind, he knew it.

Positive he was right, he quit fighting the urge, lowered his head and kissed her. Soundly.

The moment Belinda realized what Paul was going to do she closed her eyes and surrendered. They may as well have been the only two people in the world for all the attention she paid to what any passerby would think. If her hands had been free she'd have wrapped her arms around his neck and pulled him even closer.

I'm making beautiful memories, she told herself. *That's all.* She desperately wanted to be sure she'd remember Paul, above everyone else, when he was long gone.

A few more moments like this and I may remember him so well I'm ruined for any other man's kisses, she thought absently, remembering how miserable both Whitaker sisters had been over the loss of their mutual lover.

Paul deepened the kiss. The spray nozzle fell from Belinda's fingers. *I love you,* she mused. *I should tell you that. No matter how embarrassing it is for me, or how you take the news, I should tell you while I still can.*

Frightened by the insistence of her thoughts, she opened her eyes, meaning to look deeply into Paul's, to try to decide if he shared her love before she spoke out of turn and made a worse fool of herself than she already had.

The corner of her eye caught a glimpse of movement. *Gram!* Her grandmother had a shovel raised over her head like a baseball bat and was aiming for Paul's head!

Belinda tried to twist away. Staring, eyes wide with alarm, she heard Eloise warn, "Let her go, mister, or I'll scramble your brains. That is, if you've got any."

Paul straightened so fast he nearly dropped Belinda onto the grass. Staggering, he regained his balance and righted her, too. "Whoa!" he declared loudly. "This isn't what it looks like."

Eloise didn't relax her stance. "It better not be, or I'll fetch the sheriff."

Belinda hurried to relieve her of the shovel and quickly placed it out of reach. "It's okay, Gram. We were just clowning around and…"

"Didn't look to me like either one of you was foolin'. I could hardly believe my ears when Liz Finnegan phoned."

"Well, that explains a lot," Belinda said, making a face at the house across the street. "I didn't think she was even home tonight. What in the world did she tell you?"

"That there was an awful row goin' on, right in

front of your place. Said it looked like there was going to be a fight and I should get on over here as fast as I could. She didn't say anything about hanky-panky, though.''

"No, but I'm sure she will." Belinda sounded as disgusted as she felt. She looked at Paul. "I think you'd better go. If I know Liz, she's probably called the police. There's no sense in you getting involved if you don't have to be.''

He snorted. "I'm not going to leave you to deal with this alone.''

"I'm not alone. Gram is here. Go on. Go away before you get me in any more trouble.''

If she hadn't been smiling he would have been worried that she might actually be blaming him for everything that had happened. He supposed he did have to take some of the responsibility for their kiss, though it had occurred on the spur of the moment. The rest of Belinda's problems, however, had been around a lot longer than he had. And they'd still be there when he was long gone.

The idea that Belinda might change her mind and eventually reconcile with Sam—even marry him— gave Paul's gut a sharp twist. It was none of his business what she did or didn't do. Feeling out of sorts, he tried to convince himself he didn't care. He'd left Serenity once without looking back, and he intended to do it again. Soon. End of discussion.

Mustering his best look of indifference, he nodded

a polite goodbye in Belinda's direction, stuck his hands into his pockets, turned and walked away.

Belinda pulled aside the ruffled curtain and peeked out her kitchen window, watching Paul's car drive off. "Well, he's gone, Gram."

"For good, I hope."

"I don't." Belinda sighed and sat at the kitchen table across from Eloise, leaned forward and propped her chin in her hands. "I'm really going to miss him."

"Miss him? You two fight all the time."

"We don't fight. Not the way you mean, anyway. Paul and I just enjoy teasing each other."

"Is that how he got so wet tonight?" Eloise asked, one eyebrow arching.

"Ha! If you think Paul was wet, you should have seen Sam! He took a whole gallon of Snuffy's water right in the face. What a sight!"

"You didn't laugh at him in front of Paul, did you?"

"Nope. I roared," Belinda bragged, chuckling at the memory. "Don't worry. Everything worked out for the best. Sam started lecturing me about my undignified conduct and that gave me the perfect opportunity to explain how wrong he and I were for each other."

The stiffness went out of the older woman's posture, and she sagged back in her chair. "You really are serious about this, aren't you?"

"Deadly serious. I don't care if I wind up like Miss Patience or Miss Prudence. I'd rather stay single than settle for less than the man I love."

Sighing and shaking her head sadly, Eloise looked at her lovely granddaughter with tears in her eyes. "Don't."

"Don't what?"

"Don't settle. If you're sure Paul Randall is the only man for you, then you need to go after him and tell him so. If he really loves you, he'll come around."

Belinda couldn't believe the pep talk she was hearing. "Do you think it's possible? He said he hated Serenity."

"Did he say he loved you?"

"Well, no. Not in words. But I sensed it."

"Then go to him. Talk to him. Tell him how you feel. It's a calculated risk, of course, but I can see one of two things happening. Either he'll brush you off, or he'll ask you to marry him. If you love him as much as you say you do, you should be brave enough to force the issue and accept the consequences, whatever they are."

Paul didn't go straight to the Whitakers'. No place seemed like home to him anymore. Not without Belinda. It was as if she'd become such an intrinsic part of him, of his life, there was no peace or satisfaction to be found anywhere when they were apart.

He raked the fingers of one hand through his hair, pushing it back as he drove aimlessly. No matter how many times he told himself he was better off without her, he still couldn't make the idea sound plausible. Life without Belinda was life without zest, without harmony, without fulfillment.

And yet, life *with* her promised to be an impossible challenge unless she was willing to relocate to Harrison with him. He considered the probability that she might. Stranger things had happened lately. Like Aunt Pru's confession, for instance. If he'd made a thousand wild guesses he'd never have suspected that she was the culprit who set fire to the church. Or that the destruction had been accidental.

Poor Prudence. No wonder she'd always brooded so much, been so unhappy. Losing the love of your life could ruin the ensuing years and leave a person bitter. That bitterness stole whatever daily joy you did manage to find.

Like losing Belinda, Paul told himself. Did she love him? Probably. But did she love him *enough?* That was the most important question. If he didn't ask it, he'd never know, would he? Maybe in the morning he'd…

No. Now, his heart and soul insisted. *Don't wait. Go to her now.*

"I can't go like this," Paul argued, looking down at his damp, wrinkled shirt. "And if I go home and change it'll be awfully late."

It's already ten years late, you dolt, his subconscious countered. *A few more minutes won't matter.*

Belinda's hair was still damp from her shower. She'd wrapped a towel around her head like a turban and was sitting on the couch in her robe when there was a knock at the door. Snuffy, who'd been napping at her feet, came off the floor running, howling and barking.

Cautious, Belinda quieted the dog, then called through the locked door, "Who is it?"

"Me. Let me in."

"Paul?" Her heart threatened to gallop out of her chest. "I can't. I'm not dressed."

"Well, *get* dressed," he ordered. "We have to talk."

"Maybe in the morning." She heard him start to pace and talk to himself. From the tone of his mutterings, she decided it was just as well that she couldn't make out most of what he was saying. Worried, she eased open the door a crack and peeked at him. He'd changed to dry clothes but he still looked pretty frazzled.

The moment he spied her eye peeking through the slit he bent to her level and stared, his gaze narrowing. "Not in the morning. Now. Unless you want me to camp on your porch all night and give your nosy neighbors something else to gossip about."

"Okay. Stay right there," Belinda told him. "Don't go away. I'll be out in a jiffy." She slammed the door and ran for her bedroom, almost tripping over Snuffy as the little beagle joined in the exciting game her mistress was evidently playing.

Giddy beyond belief, Belinda talked aloud. "What in the world am I going to wear? It's not fair! This is all happening too soon. My hair isn't dry and I haven't had enough time to rehearse my speech! And, and…"

Frantic, she began to toss outfits onto her bed, rejecting each tentative choice. *Something not too fancy and not too casual. Appealing but not too sexy.*

She finally settled on a simple white sheath, dislodging the towel when she pulled the dress over her head. Her hair was a damp, tangled mess. She'd prayed for the chance to see Paul again, but not when she looked like *this*. How did the Lord expect her to make a good enough impression to convince the poor man she'd be the perfect choice for his wife when she looked like a drowned rat?

Stopping in the middle of her bedroom, Belinda spread her hands wide, closed her eyes, took a deep breath and consciously gave her will over to God. "Okay. I prayed about it and You sent him, Father. This is Your party. You run it, and I'll try to stay out of Your way." A slight smile lifted the corners of her mouth as she added, "I might need a little help with that part, but then You already know that, don't You?"

The sense of peace she got from her prayer stayed

with her until she reached the front door, opened it and saw the look of anguish and longing on Paul's face. Then he reached for her, cupped her cheek with his palm, and she forgot all about her promise to God.

Dreamy-eyed, Belinda moved her head against his hand to encourage his caress as she slipped her arms around his waist. "I'm so glad you came back."

"Are you?"

She nodded. "Uh-huh. I was going to come looking for you in the morning, anyway."

"You were?"

Paul's lips were so near to hers when he spoke, she could feel the warmth of his breath, imagine the sweetness of his kiss once more. Everything was going to be all right. She could feel it all the way to her toes. "Yes. I didn't want you to get away from me again." Raising her gaze to his, she gathered her courage and whispered, "I love you too much to let you go without putting up a fight."

Relieved beyond belief, Paul took her face in both hands, his thumbs caressing her cheeks, his eyes growing misty with suppressed emotion. There was hope, after all. This was their second chance. The answer to his fondest dreams. He was older. Wiser. And he now had the resources to make Belinda happy, if she'd only let him. He took the chance she would.

"There's one way to guarantee that we'll always be together," he murmured.

Belinda stared at him, her lips parted, her brain whirling. Could he mean what she thought he meant, what she wanted him to mean? Or was her vivid imagination playing tricks on her again? She had to ask. "How?"

"Simple. You marry me."

Time stopped while Belinda struggled to believe what she was hearing. Could it be that her prayers had been answered so fast, so miraculously? It was Paul's look of happy expectation that finally convinced her how serious he was.

Ecstatic, she threw herself at him and kissed him with all the fervor she'd been saving for the man she would one day wed. "Oh, Paul! Yes, yes, yes. I love you so much!"

Years of unfulfilled longing, suddenly freed, surged from his subconscious, threatening to overwhelm him. Belinda, his Belinda, had just agreed to be his wife!

Breathing hard, Paul yearned to sweep her in his arms and carry her off like a princess being liberated from a dungeon. He realized he'd have to take immediate charge of the situation before they *both* got carried away by their mutual passion. It was that or say goodbye to what remained of his tenuous self-control and be sorry later.

He pulled her arms from around him, drew her hands against his chest and forced himself to step back. The love shining in her eyes was the most beautiful sight he'd ever seen. Happily, all the plans he'd made when he'd thought he was merely entertaining a foolish daydream about their future together could be put to real use.

Smiling, he said, "You won't have to worry about a thing, honey. I've already got most of our problems figured out. I'm not very well connected in the real estate business, in spite of my work on my aunts' behalf, so we will need to find a good Realtor."

"Sure. Fine," she agreed sweetly. What a joy it was to picture him as a permanent part of her everyday life! What a blessing. It was amazing how quickly Paul's attitude about living in Serenity had changed. Love could do that, she supposed. To think that he was willing to give up everything just to make her happy!

"Good." He placed a tender kiss on her forehead. "I'm not sure how good the market is right now. If your place doesn't sell right away we can probably rent it. My condo in Harrison is plenty big enough for both of us."

Belinda's hopes crashed in a whirl of jumbled emotion. "*What* did you say?"

"I was talking about my condo." Paul started to frown. "Uh-oh. I just remembered. The rules don't allow dogs. I'll bet Eloise would keep Snuffy for you until..."

"Whoa!" She flattened her palms on his chest and firmly pushed him away. "What are you talking about? I'm not selling my house. And I'm certainly not giving my *dog* away." She stared at Paul as if seeing him for the first time. "How could you even ask such a thing?"

"Because it's the most logical option," he said, puzzled by her strong negative reaction. "At least for now. Your house is way too small. I need room for a home office with a computer, fax, copier...you know."

"Not to mention the fact that my place also happens to be located in Serenity?"

He didn't argue. "That, too. Of course."

Other serious complications were beginning to occur to Belinda now that she'd stopped being so overwhelmed by her runaway emotions. "What about my job? Have you thought of that?"

Paul slipped an arm around her shoulders and tried to pull her to his side. To his surprise, she resisted. "Don't worry about working. I told you I'd take care of you." Amused at her standoffish attitude and the childish scowl on her face, he chuckled. "You've got to stop seeing me as the penniless kid who begged you to run away with him on the back of his motorbike."

"This isn't about *money!*" She was so incensed, so disappointed, she grabbed his wrist and whipped his arm off her shoulders so she could face him squarely. "It's about caring what the other person thinks. You never even asked me if I wanted to leave Serenity."

"You know how I feel about this town. You

couldn't have thought I'd agree to live *here*." Paul had to fight to keep his voice calm. Clearly, his expectations of recapturing their lost love and building a secure future with Belinda had been overly optimistic.

"Why not?" she shouted. "You want to drag me to Harrison where I don't know a soul. How is that any better?"

"Well, for starters, nobody there hates your guts," Paul countered, trying to get her to appreciate the dissimilarity of their situations. She was free to go anywhere, do anything, while he was tied to a law practice that had taken years to build. It was a four-hour round-trip commute to Harrison, half of it on winding, two-lane roads. Even if he were willing to consider such an idiotic daily schedule, the long, tedious drives would leave him so worn out he'd be lucky to be awake during the day, let alone intellectually keen enough to do his clients any good.

Sighing with resignation, he said, "I can see I've made a big mistake. You care more about this town than you do about me. Why don't we just forget I said anything about marriage. It would never work."

She wanted to shout. To argue. To contradict him. But she couldn't. Paul was right. There was no way to refute his disheartening conclusions. Biting her lower lip so she wouldn't start to cry and make a fool of herself, Belinda folded her arms across her chest in a posture guaranteed to protect what little was left of her pride. "Don't worry," she said with as much rancor as she could muster, "I won't sue you for breach of promise. I don't know a good lawyer."

With a snort of disgust, he wheeled and stalked off the porch. Belinda's heart was breaking. How could he just give up and walk away like that? Didn't he love her enough to at least try to work out their differences?

Suddenly, she realized what crucial ingredient had been missing from Paul's marriage proposal. He'd planned the details of their future, all right, but he hadn't said the words that might have made it all work.

He'd never told her he loved her. Not once.

Chapter Thirteen

Belinda moped around for the next week and a half. The only one she confided in was Snuffy, and that was simply because the dog could never repeat anything that might reveal how badly she ached to be with Paul in spite of everything that had gone wrong between them.

Guilt was one of her biggest problems. In the course of praying for enlightenment, she realized she'd blamed Paul for not considering her side of their impasse while doing *exactly* the same thing to him.

In contrast, Sheila was delivering daily reports on her budding romance with Sam. Belinda was genuinely happy about that. If Sam had been grieving over their breakup she'd have felt responsible for his unhappiness, too.

She was sitting on her porch steps, enjoying the cool evening air and scratching Snuffy's droopy ears, when her grandmother strolled up with a cheery greeting. "Hi, honey."

"Hi, Gram." Belinda eyed the older woman's empty hands. "No cookies?"

"Not today." Eloise tested the dirt in the flower bed with the toe of her sneaker. "Your snapdragons are thirsty."

"Probably."

"Hmm." She plopped down on the porch beside Belinda. "So. Have you had any word from Paul Randall lately?"

"No." To fill the heavy silence Belinda asked, "Why? Have you?" When Eloise surprised her by saying yes, she whipped around so fast she nearly slid off the step. "You have? What? When? Is the Whitaker deal closed?"

"If you mean, is Paul coming back here to take care of the contract the way we all thought he would, no."

Belinda's heart lodged in her throat. "No?" The word barely squeaked out beside it.

"No. Pru says the escrow company was able to fax all the necessary papers to his office for his approval. It doesn't look like he'll have to visit Serenity at all."

Staring into the distance, focusing on nothing, Belinda sensed the intensity of Eloise's questioning gaze. It made her feel like a bug trapped under a microscope. Or a kid with a sinful secret. Telling the dog her private thoughts had helped ease her conscience to begin with but she could see it was time to confide in a real person.

"When I told Paul how I felt about him he did ask me to marry him, just like I'd hoped," she confessed.

"Why didn't you *tell* me? When did this happen?"

"The night before he left."

"Well, well." Eloise's initial grin faded as she took note of her granddaughter's solemn expression. "You don't seem very happy. You didn't turn him down, did you?"

"No. Actually, I said yes." Sniffing quietly in self-contempt, Belinda shook her head. "But that was before he told me he wanted me to sell my house and go away with him."

"Excuse me?" Eloise scowled. "What's wrong with that?"

"Nothing. Everything." Throwing herself backward, Belinda rested her upper body on the porch floor, cradled her head in her hands and stared at the pink-tinged clouds of early evening. "He never even asked me what I wanted to do, Gram. He just told me how it was going to be."

"And you contradicted him with loving understanding and Christian forbearance, like the Good Book says, right?"

"Not exactly."

"Oh?" Eloise smiled indulgently. "What *did* you say?"

"I don't have a clue. I've gone back over that scene so many times, rehearsing what I *should* have said, I can't tell fact from fiction anymore."

"Well, since Paul's left and you haven't heard a word from him, I take it the outcome was not good."

Sitting up, Belinda made a throaty sound of derision. "Humpf. No kidding. If he'd just asked my opinion instead of telling me what to do..."

"You'd have told *him* what to do."

"Well, yes." Pulling a face, she let her frustration show. "I've lived in Serenity all my life. You're here. All my friends are here. Momma and Daddy are buried here. This is my life."

"It is so far," Eloise said wisely. "The question is, are you going to play it safe and turn into a hermit like poor Prudence or are you going to trust the Lord, step out on faith and meet your future head-on?"

"I always trust God," Belinda insisted.

"As long as you're comfortable, you do. Most of us are like that. It's when we're troubled or confused that our true nature shows. You were perfectly willing to support harmony and forgiveness between Pru and her sister, but you're not ready to do the same for yourself."

"Do you think I should leave Serenity? Is that what you're saying?" Tears rimmed her eyes.

Eloise put a motherly arm around her grand-daughter's shoulders. "Not necessarily. I'm not the one who has to decide what's most important to you. You are." She leaned closer to kiss her on the cheek. "Have you prayed about whether or not you should leave here to be with Paul?"

The truth hit Belinda like a bolt of lightning on an otherwise sunny day. She'd asked God for help and strength and a lot of other things lately, including Paul Randall's love on a silver platter, but she'd failed to ask for the Lord's *advice*. "Um, no. Not exactly."

"And why is that, do you suppose?"

"Probably because I don't want to get an answer I don't like," Belinda admitted softly, reluctantly.

"You *are* getting smarter in your old age," Eloise teased. "Just remember, whatever you decide, I'm on your side. I think Paul is, too."

"He sure had a funny way of showing it."

Laughing, Eloise shook her head. "I'll bet if I asked him, he'd say the same thing about you."

Paul was determined to forget what a fool he'd been to propose to Belinda. Forgetting was a good idea. A logical idea. Only the harder he tried to put her out of his mind, the more his heart magnified the love that made forgetting impossible.

It took him ten days to narrow his choices down to only two. Simply put, he could either do things her way or let her go. After finally hurdling the worst barriers to their happiness and proving his innocence, letting her go was unthinkable. So was resigning himself to a lifetime spent in Serenity.

Grumbling, Paul stalked out to his car and slid behind the wheel, then sat there for a moment, thinking. He could do this. He had to do this. Life with Belinda might be the most difficult challenge he'd ever accepted, but life without her was no life at all.

"I have a map to get me to Harrison and Paul's business card with his office address," Belinda told her grandmother. "Snuffy's dry dog food is in the big plastic can next to the washing machine. As long as she has plenty of water she can stay out in my back yard during the day, even in hot weather. Just don't forget to keep the gate latched."

Eloise laughed. "I won't. Don't worry about us. We always get along fine. I'll even take her home with me and let her help me bake some doggie cookies if she gets bored."

"I'm glad I won't be here to see that," Belinda said, rolling her eyes.

"Take all the time you need. No hurry coming back."

"I'm not going to throw myself at the man, if that's what you mean." Belinda glanced at the load of personal possessions filling the back seat of her car. "First I'll rent my own place so he doesn't get the wrong idea about why I'm there. After that, we'll see."

"I certainly hope so," her grandmother said. "You deserve a dose of happiness."

"I don't deserve Paul. Not after the awful way I snapped at him. I wasn't seeing things from his point of view at all."

"I'm sure he'll understand when you explain it to him." She kissed Belinda's cheek and gave her a hug. "Now, get out of here before I start to boo hoo and spoil your trip."

I'm doing the right thing, Belinda insisted. Waving goodbye to the dearest person in the world, she started for Harrison and a confrontation with her future.

Correction. Gram was the *second* dearest person in the world. The dearest one was an attractive, stubborn man who was going to listen to her apology if she had to hog-tie him to make him sit still long enough. And while he was at it, he'd better admit he loved her, too, or else.

Paul went straight to Belinda's as soon as he hit town. No familiar barking greeted his arrival. Walking all the way around the house, he peeked in the windows.

"Might as well give up." The woman's shrill voice came from across the street. "She's gone."

He shaded his eyes with his hand so he could see the informant as he started to his car. "Where did she go?"

"Don't know. At least that noisy dog of hers is gone, too. Hoo-whee. What a blessing."

That news brought him up short. Belinda had been furious when he'd suggested she leave Snuffy with Eloise until they could find a place that allowed pets. If she'd taken the dog with her when she left, that might mean she wasn't coming back!

Frowning, Paul got into his car and sped toward Eloise's. Talk about illogical. Why would Belinda suddenly decide to leave Serenity when her attachment to the town was the very reason she'd gotten so upset with him?

Belinda had planned to choose an apartment and reinforce her decision to move before she contacted Paul. By the time she reached Harrison, however, she'd had so much time to think, to imagine his reaction when she told him about it, she couldn't bear to wait any longer.

Finding his office was easy. Making herself enter was a lot harder. "Okay, Father," she whispered. "I'm here. I know this is the right thing to do. I'm trusting You to take it from here."

Straightening her spine and resolving to persevere no matter what, she pulled open the heavy glass door and walked in. The waiting room was impressive, sparsely furnished yet elegantly simple in muted tones of beige and gray.

A middle-aged receptionist looked up from her desk behind a low counter. "May I help you?"

"Yes. Paul Randall, please."

"I'm sorry," the woman said. "Mr. Randall is out."

Belinda's hopes fell. "Oh." Obviously, the Lord wanted her to see to the mundane details of her life, as she'd originally planned, before she encountered Paul again. Disappointed, she said, "I see. Then I guess I should make an appointment. How soon will he be back?"

"I'm sorry. I can't say." The receptionist picked up a pen and paper. "Would you like to leave a message?"

"Yes. Tell him Ms. Carnes has decided to move to Harrison. Permanently."

"Carnes? Belinda Carnes?"

She smiled, gratified to have her name recognized. "That's me. I don't have a place here yet. I'll phone you with my new address as soon as I'm settled."

"But…"

The smile faded. "What's the matter? Did Paul tell you not to let me in?"

"No. Oh, no," the woman said. "Nothing like that. It's just that…he's gone to see *you*."

"Me? Where? When?"

"He left this morning."

"So did I!" Belinda was ecstatic. "We must have passed each other on the road."

"Probably. I assume you came by highway 412.

Since that's the shortest route, Mr. Randall would logically have used it, too.''

"No doubt. He's so sensible he drives me up the wall! Thanks!'' Laughing to herself, Belinda dashed out the door. Paul had gone to *her!* Praise the Lord! It was a miracle. A happy future was waiting for her at home. Nothing mattered but getting there.

Paul banged on Eloise's door harder than he'd intended. Startled, Snuffy let out a series of whoops that echoed through the house. Hearing that, Paul began to pray that Belinda was inside, too.

Eloise jerked open the door. When she saw who her visitor was, her jaw dropped. "What are *you* doing here?''

"Looking for Belinda.'' Snuffy was spinning in tight circles at his feet. "When she wasn't home, I thought…''

Eloise burst into laughter. "This is hilarious. She went to see *you!*''

"Me? Where?''

"In Harrison.'' Shaking her head, she chuckled softly. "You two are really something, you know that? I told her to call you first and tell you she was on her way but she insisted it had to be a surprise. Sure looks like it was.''

Stunned, Paul caught his breath. "Why did she leave Snuffy behind?''

"Because she wasn't sure she'd be able to find an apartment that allowed dogs. This is not a permanent arrangement, believe me. I'm more of a cat person, like your aunt." Sobering, she asked, "Did you stop in to see Pru? She's really been worried about you ever since you found out the church fire was her fault. She's afraid you'll hold it against her forever."

"There was a time when I might have," Paul said. "But not anymore. Belinda once told me it's a lot easier to look back and see how God has worked in the past than it is to figure out His plans for the present. She was sure right."

"Or His plans for the future," Eloise offered. "So, what happens now?"

"I go find Belinda." Paul was grinning. "If she calls, ask her where she's staying, get a phone number where I can reach her and tell her I'm on my way!"

Paul was nearly to Mountain Home before it occurred to him to alert his office. He had to wait until he'd driven out of the steepest hills before he could get a steady connection on his cellular phone. The receptionist answered on the first ring. "Randall and Associates."

"Alice," he said, wheeling around a sharp turn, "it's Paul. I want you to be on the lookout for Belinda Carnes." The phone connection faded, crackled, then strengthened slightly. If he didn't know better he'd think he'd heard Alice giggling behind the static. "What?"

"I said, it's too late, boss. The lady's been here."

Paul's heart did a flip and landed in his throat. "That's terrific! Did she leave a number?"

"No. I got the impression she might have changed her mind about sticking around, though, since you were gone. It wouldn't surprise me if she was on her way home. Just stay put in Serenity. I'll bet she shows up."

Tucking the phone between his chin and shoulder, he two-handed a sharp curve. "It's a little late for that. I've already started home. I'm almost to Cotter."

This time, Paul was certain he heard his secretary chuckling quietly before she said, "That should be perfect. Ms. Carnes ran out of here about an hour ago. If she's in as big a hurry as I think she is, you two should be passing each other right about now."

"If we haven't already." Paul put down the phone, slowed and began to scan oncoming traffic, hoping to spot Belinda's car among all the others approaching.

At this point, he could either turn around and go back or continue in the direction he'd been going. If Belinda had stayed in Harrison, that was where he wanted to be. On the other hand, if Alice's guess was right, he needed to head for Serenity. Without more concrete information there was no way to make a logical decision.

Totally frustrated, Paul muttered under his breath.

Driving in aimless circles wouldn't accomplish a thing except to burn gasoline.

Continuing to study the traffic, he noticed that one car was going much faster than the others. It whizzed by him in a blur. Could it be?

His pulse sped. His breath caught. He had only the witness of his heart that it was Belinda he'd seen behind the wheel of the car. That was enough.

Cutting across the grass median without concern for what the rough terrain might do to his car, Paul floored the accelerator and raced after her.

Belinda glanced in the rearview mirror. Two cars were rapidly closing on her. One was black, like Paul's. The other was white with a light bar fastened across its roof. The lights were flashing red and blue!

"I shouldn't have promised God I wouldn't speed," she murmured, slowing and changing lanes so she'd be ready to pull to the shoulder of the road if the state trooper was after her instead of the black car. She kept her eyes on the colored lights. As soon as the black car passed, the patrol car fell in behind her and blinked its headlights.

Shaking with nervousness, Belinda obediently pulled over. There was no good excuse for her excess speed. No reason the trooper should be lenient. She gritted her teeth. This was going to be one whopper of a ticket. The worst part was, she deserved it. Resigned to her fate, she unfastened her seat belt and climbed out of the car.

The approaching officer touched the flat wide brim of his hat. "Ma'am. Do you know how fast you were going?"

Belinda shook her head. "No, sir. I'm afraid I don't have a clue. You see, I was on my way—" She broke off and turned to follow his gaze when she saw him scowl and lean his head to one side to peer past her.

The black car had also pulled over and was rapidly backing toward them along the wide shoulder of the road. It skidded to a stop in front of her car. The driver's door swung open.

Belinda shrieked, "Paul!" and took off running, leaving the startled officer standing alone. Arms held wide, she smacked into Paul's chest with such force he staggered backward before grabbing her and using her momentum to swing her around, feet off the ground.

"Oh, Paul! I went to your office and they said—"

"I know." He was alternately raining kisses over her face, nuzzling her neck and laughing. "I was at *your* house."

Forgetting everything else, Belinda clung to him and kissed him until they were both breathless, then slid her cheek next to his. "Your face is all scratchy."

"I guess I forgot to shave this morning. I had a lot on my mind."

"Oh? What would that be?"

"I was busy deciding to give up everything for the woman I love."

Love? Yippee! He'd finally admitted it! Belinda was grinning so broadly her smile muscles hurt. "What a coincidence. I just gave up everything for some guy who lives in Harrison. I sure hope he's worth it."

Paul cupped her face in his hands and gazed deeply into her eyes. "I'll do my very best never to disappoint you."

Before Belinda could reply, she heard the gruff sound of a throat being cleared behind her. *Close* behind her. She gasped and whirled, staying as close to Paul as she could. "Uh-oh. Sorry, Officer. You slipped my mind." It was a relief to see him nod and stifle a smile.

"I can see that." Looking at Paul, he asked, "You two have a fight or something?"

"More of a misunderstanding," Paul said. He wrapped his arms around Belinda. "Everything's going to be fine now."

The officer snorted. "Not if you two keep distracting other drivers. You've almost caused at least three traffic accidents since I stopped you." His smile grew. With a nod toward their cars, he said, "Go on. Get out of here before I run you both in for kissing on the highway."

Belinda glanced at Paul. "Is that against the law?"

"It is if our friend with the badge says it is." He kept one arm around her waist and urged her toward the Lexus. "Come on. Let's go somewhere more private. We have a lot to talk about."

The officer stopped them. "Hold it. You can't leave her car here. The off-ramp to Cotter is up ahead about a mile." He pointed. "Now go on. Git. Both of you."

Carefully driving below the speed limit, Belinda led the way with Paul right behind. To her great relief, the trooper stayed on the highway when she and Paul turned off.

Parts of Cotter looked even older than Serenity. The newer portion lay nearest the highway. The rest of the town, perched on a picturesque bluff, could be reached by way of a quaint historic bridge over the White River.

Stopping at the river access because it was the first available place to pull off the road, Belinda parked and ran back to Paul. He gave her a brief hug, took her hand and led the way to a secluded patch of shade near the quietly meandering river. "I'll manage okay in Serenity," he said. "It's worth it to be with you."

"No, no. I'm moving to Harrison." She was shaking her head vigorously. "I've already decided. I can get a job almost anywhere. You don't have that option. I wasn't thinking clearly before."

"Uh-uh. You'd hate it there. Then you'd start to hate me. I won't let you do it."

Belinda pulled away and stepped back, her fists planted firmly on her hips. "*Let* me? You won't *let* me?"

"Bad choice of words," Paul admitted ruefully. "What I should have said is that it's not as important to me where we live. You have friends in Serenity. Folks you've known all your life. I won't ask you to give that up."

Impressed by his sincerity and evident love, she smiled with new awareness and spoke softly, sweetly. "Guess what the sermon was about last Sunday, Paul? Neighbors. And do you know who the Bible says our neighbors are? *Everybody.* I'd never thought of it that way before, had you?"

"And your point is?" One eyebrow arched quizzically.

"Hearing that lesson preached was the direct answer to my prayers. It finalized the change I needed to make in my outlook. Sure, I'll miss Serenity and Gram and all my friends, but we can make a good life wherever we go. Real neighbors are everywhere." She swept her arm in a wide arc. "Even right here in Cotter."

Suddenly struck by the significance of what she'd said, Belinda scanned the area. Most of the houses on the bluff above were painted white and nestled amid massive shade trees, making the scene look as ideal as a picture postcard.

She paused to clear her head and gather her thoughts, then took a deep, settling breath. "Paul? Are you thinking what I'm thinking?"

"In this case, I may be," he said cautiously. "This town is about halfway between both our places. You could visit your grandmother pretty easily, and it wouldn't take me as long to drive to work, either."

"And it's gorgeous here!" Belinda was warming to the idea. "We'd both have to start over, too, so it would be a fair compromise. It's perfect!"

"Does this mean the wedding is on?" he asked, grinning.

"I don't know. You took back your last proposal."

"I could always make up a new one."

Belinda was so happy she thought she'd burst. "You'd better, or I'll... I'll get my grandmother to hunt you down and conk you with her shovel."

Paul pulled her into his arms and held her close until he stopped laughing. "In that case, will you marry me?"

"Snuffy comes, too," she informed him amiably. "I already promised her she could."

"Okay. But she gets her own room. I've waited ten years for you and I'm not about to share."

Overflowing with joy, Belinda agreed. "It's a deal. Come on. Let's tour the town and go house shopping. The Lord went to a lot of trouble to bring us here. I don't want to disappoint Him."

"In a minute. I have something I want to do first." Pulling her close, Paul lowered his head and sealed their engagement with a long, slow kiss.

Belinda surrendered the last shred of her misgivings as she kissed him back. Overflowing with joy, she wanted to sing, to shout, to tell everyone who'd listen that Paul Randall was the most awesome, the most wonderful answer to prayer she'd ever received.

It didn't matter that it had taken ten years to happen. He was one answer that was *definitely* worth waiting for.

*   *   *   *   *

Be sure to pick up Valerie Hansen's next Love Inspired, coming in Fall 2001.

Dear Reader,

Everything that happens to us changes us. It's easy to notice the catastrophic events and acknowledge their immense influence, yet often it's the accumulation of the little things that makes us who we are. What we are.

Every day we're faced with difficulties and choose how we will ultimately react to them. As life goes on and those reactions become a deep-seated part of our character, we can be fooled into believing we've lost our ability to choose joy over sorrow, gain over loss, forgiveness over anger.

When Jesus said, "Blessed are the peacemakers, for they shall be called the children of God," I think He was referring to those special people who, with love and patient understanding, can open our eyes to the blessings of forgiving...beginning with forgiving ourselves for our own mistakes.

No one can go back and undo the past. But we can put it behind us, give the remainder of our lives to Jesus, ask for God's perfect forgiveness and begin again.

Every breath, every heartbeat, every moment, is a gift from God. Whether we look for reasons to celebrate that gift or bury it in bitterness is up to us.

I'd love to hear from you! If you'd like a personal reply or notification of my upcoming books, please include a self-addressed, stamped envelope. You can write to me at: Valerie Hansen, P.O. Box 13, Glencoe, AR 72539-0013.

Blessings!

Valerie Hansen

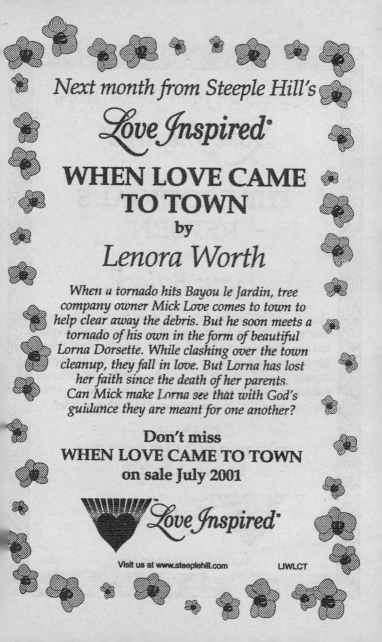

Next month from Steeple Hill's

Love Inspired®

THE PRODIGAL'S RETURN
by
Lynn Bulock

Widow Laurel Collins decides to move from California to Missouri with her teenage son to be closer to her family, but she never expects her life to turn upside down! When her son gets picked up for skateboarding by the handsome deputy sheriff, Tripp Jordan, the sparks fly between Laurel and Tripp. Can a prodigal daughter and a by-the-book lawman find common ground in faith and love?

**Don't miss
THE PRODIGAL'S RETURN
On sale July 2001**

Love Inspired®

Next month
from Steeple Hill's

Love Inspired

HEAVEN SENT
by
Jillian Hart

*Successful photographer Hope Ashton comes home to
Montana to care for her grandmother and encounters old
flame Matthew Shaw, a widower raising triplet sons. Soon
Matthew's mother and Hope's grandmother are hatching a
plan to bring them together. With lives as different as day
and night, will they discover that their love for God and
each other can bring them together?*

**Don't miss
HEAVEN SENT
On sale July 2001**

Love Inspired